ESMARELDA

What does it feel like?

BUTCH

(finds his shirt)
What does what feel like?

ESMARELDA

Killing a man. Beating another man to death with your bare hands.

Butch pulls on his tee-shirt.

BUTCH

Are you some kinda weirdo?

ESMARELDA

No, it's a subject I have much interest in. You are the first
person I ever met who has killed somebody. So, what was it like to
kill a man? . . .

BUTCH

-- I couldn't tell ya. I didn't know he was dead 'til you told me
he was dead. Now I know he's dead, do you wanna know
how I feel about it?

Esmarelda nods her head: "yes."

BUTCH

I don't feel the least little bit bad.

Quentin Tarantino, *Pulp Fiction*

Singapore

Singapore

by

Eva Aldea

www.hhousebooks.com

Eddie 2005-2018
Cassie 2005-2012
Soy Sauce 2008-2020

Hardback ISBN: 978-1-910688-84-7

Cover design by Ken Dawson

Typeset by Julia B. Lloyd

Published in the UK

Holland House Books

Holland House

47 Greenham Road

Newbury, Berkshire RG14 7HY

United Kingdom

www.hhousebooks.com

Somehow, the old boy gets lucky.

She stares at the ground. The small body is moving slowly and agonisingly, dying but not fast enough. She looks up at the horizon. The air is clear, and the sky is blue and high. The green expanse below her stretches to the white symmetry of the old naval college, a band of glittering water beyond, and then the rising grey steel and glass. And yet these things take up almost no space, none of the air that she is breathing. Cool in her lungs, but the sun is still warming. That early autumn golden sunlight floods the void, fills it with a syrupy glow, covers everything with an intangible viscosity, seems to slow everything down, trap things, like flies in amber. A plane in the sky, white, tiny, seems stuck in the infinite blue.

The faraway aircraft makes her feel so deeply sad, and yet there is nothing, nothing at all, apart from this moment. Nothing more beautiful or perfect than here, breathing in the sunshine, standing above her city, this moment. 'Isn't this a splendid view?' she says to her dogs, they oblivious, more interested in smells and now the recent prey. A specimen destined for extinction, slower or stupider, is caught in the old dog's maw. He loses interest, drops it, pricks his ears up again when the squirrel twitches, picks it up and shakes it, but without heart.

She walks here almost every day. They know it well, she and the two hounds. A fantasy of medieval royalty, the palace, the hunt; now, a coffee at the cart by the observatory. As they walk down the gully where the squirrels live, the dogs are excited, hold their heads high and their bodies taut. The air, clear and golden to her, must be awash with scents and secrets to them. She can only watch their bodies receive these messages: twitching noses, turning ears, then a cocked head, a paw raised on the ready. But they are sighthounds, so it is the flutter of a furry tail above the grass that sets them off, from still to leaping in no time at all, paws thundering like hooves on the ground – she loves that sound, feels it in her chest through her own feet. She loves the sight of their bodies in flight, the double suspension rotary gallop, only sighthounds and cheetahs hunt by this fastest and most explosive of gaits, where the body is in touch with the ground only a quarter of the time. The rest is spent flying. Closing the gap between predator and prey at a great expenditure of energy. They run fast, greyhounds, but tire quickly. Spend most of the day conserving energy for the hunt, like big cats. Lazy we say, give them their bowl of kibble of an evening. But the forces exerted by a greyhound running can snap tendons and break bones, only luck decides if those are of the hunter or the prey. They don't usually catch anything here, too many trees, the squirrels are too nimble. Often they limp back, a torn stopper pad, a knocked up toe. Usually nothing serious, she worries that one day something serious, but this is their most alive. Watching them hunt makes her feel alive. She couldn't stop them hunting, for their sake, for her sake.

She can't just leave the dying squirrel. She feels responsible, it was her animal that did this, it is in her power to end this. It is her duty to stop this suffering. She has no gloves on, it is still too warm out, and she doesn't want to touch, get scratched or bitten. She stands on the squirrel's head, but the turf is soft, it sinks beneath her foot. She digs the toe and side of the shoe into the squirrel's neck, trying to dislocate the vertebrae. Pushing hard, she thinks she feels a kind of pop, finally the creature is still, and something pinkish is coming out of its nose. It must be brain, the head is quite shapeless now. The squirrel has to be dead now. She moves away, looks away, feeling a little sick. It was the right thing to do.

Aeroplanes in clear blue skies have taken on a new meaning in the last few weeks. For as long as she can remember the hum of a plane overhead on a sunny day has made her feel sad and lonely. When the air is clear and you lift your head to see the glint of steel up ahead, you notice the immense void that surrounds every human being. Now, squinting up at the passing plane as she walks to work, she imagines herself inside, being taken away, leaving London beneath and behind. The skyscrapers and neon lights of Asian megalopolises lie ahead, shifting florescent blues and reds seen through grey glass, moving in the night.

The last lecture, the usual thinning clientele at the end of term. She can see that girl asleep in the back row. Banked seating is not a great hiding place, don't they realise? The scribblers up front and the variations of vacancy in between. But she knows she can rouse them, she is a good speaker, she'll get them to smile and learn without realising it themselves. Anecdotes are her secret weapon, hidden missiles finding their way into unsuspecting brains and detonating their charge of knowledge, now or perhaps much later. She remembers the sense herself, suddenly understanding what a teacher said years down the line, when re-reading something a second or even a third time. The key is to make them listen, but she's been blessed with a loud voice, many times she has been told to shush but it comes into its own now, and in noisy pubs too. It wakes everyone up, except that girl at the back.

She talks, and leans on the pulpit and clicks the slides forward and sips her coffee and takes a walk and scribbles on the board. Some would say it is a performance, and often it starts like that, with a script. But when she gets to a point of explanation, and these days she leaves blanks in her lecture notes for these, it is as if she is face to face with the one person it is crucial to explain this point to, make that person, just them, understand. And she needs to adapt her explanation to make them all understand, all two hundred of them (although less at this time of year), so she tells the story two or three ways, straight and complicated and the funny way with metaphors that appear to her like visions to a saint. She sees the more outlandish versions reflected back in knitted brows, and sometimes smirks, but they're listening and that is half the battle won.

Today it is Baudrillard's simulacra that need the treatment. They've heard of the desert of the real, *The Matrix* has gone from exciting new thing to an old cult classic in the years since she wrote this lecture. They're all wrong, of course, there is nothing post-apocalyptic or dusty about the desert of the real. No, it is the all singing and all dancing colour show that is late capitalism, once you'd say Kodachrome, now its 4k HD or is it 8k, already? Even the grandest of productions are revealed as the soap operas they are by a 200Hz refresh rate. If your wildest dreams look too real, how can you tell a copy from a reproduction? Before the real was coded, it was manufactured in cities sprung from the union of Philip K. Dick and Ridley Scott's imaginations. Maybe a high definition memory is the surest sign of a real that no longer exists. The reflections of neon in rain-slicked pavements flicker through her mind in old fashioned 24 frames per second, and she reflects on the modern orientalism of her imagined destination. She has an origami unicorn which she places carefully at the front of the pulpit at the start of the lecture each year. This year she leaves it behind. The move is finally starting to feel real.

Is there any residential street in London on which a lorry carrying a forty foot container could comfortably park? she wonders as the corrugated grey box with MAERSK stencilled on the side squeezes down their narrow cul-de-sac. It doesn't look like it will, but it goes, after much head-scratching and shouting and the lifting of a motorbike chained to a lamppost outside the house. The dogs have gone to kennels, awaiting their veterinary sign-off before being loaded as cargo on a plane following her own by forty-eight hours, so the house feels empty already, even before the men descend on it and start packing everything up. They watch as their possession are wrapped, taped, boxed; made into pupae of varied sizes, like the square eggs of some strange alien breed.

Outside it is a sunny, hot day, and some friends come around. Together they peer into the as yet empty container, and opening the door with a clang to let the light in, gingerly climb up, venture in, nose around the space that will convey their stuff across the sea. It is much too big for their possessions, the furniture could all fit in there and still leave room for the car, but that's not allowed, along with firewood. They ponder why firewood cannot be transported in a shipping container to Singapore, if one should wish do so, but why would anyone want firewood in tropical heat? Somebody brings beers and snacks and they all sit down inside the container and have a picnic until it gets too hot and they sit on the wall at the front of the house instead and watch the first of the boxes being loaded.

It is not until later that night, trying to sleep in the bed left behind in a house full of cardboard cocoons, that she wonders whether anyone had suffocated in the container they had their farewell party in, or whether containers in which people have died get taken out of commission, put to better uses. It is ironic, she thinks, how one of the central instruments of global capitalism gets recycled and touted as ecologically and socially redemptive housing. Pests, she also thinks, that's why no firewood: invasive species.

The next day is the last day; in the evening they leave. The bed gets packed and loaded onto the lorry, along with any remaining boxes.

The house empties out, fills with dust and light. Only their suitcases are left. Her in-laws come and take them out for lunch and drive them to the airport. They're far too early for their eleven pm flight, but it's business so they can while away the time in the lounge. It is the first time she has flown business class long-haul. As they get on the plane and make themselves comfortable, the space, the flat bed, the nifty little storage lockers and the noise cancelling headphones make her excited like a little child. Best of all is a set of rounded white porcelain salt and pepper shakers that arrive on the dinner tray, the two pieces fit together cleverly, making a little china snowman. She desperately wants to steal it, but she doesn't dare.

1. Underfurnished

The new house is large and entirely empty. They were under the impression that the landlady had agreed to leave them a few pieces of furniture, a bed, a sofa, a table and chairs, until theirs arrive from London. It is not possible to get a specific date for this arrival, but the estimate is four to six weeks. The smaller air shipment – containing plates and cutlery, some cooking equipment, the TV – should come within a week. But they need something to sleep on. They can go back to the hotel for another night but the day after that the dogs are arriving. Although it is obvious that there has been some mistake, neither estate agent, for there are always two in Singapore, the tenant's and the landlady's, apologise. Their agent takes the initiative and drives them to a furniture rental shop across town and manages to secure them a bed, a sofa, a table and chairs, the very same day. The agent takes them to a shopping mall near their new house to buy pillows, duvet, bedclothes. She's brought towels at least.

The house is hot. They set up the bed and turn the aircon on. They have no internet connection and no TV, but there are two bars that serve food just twenty metres away at the beginning of their road, by the intersection with a small road of shops. They have a cold beer in the evening, something to eat. It feels like a holiday in a strange hotel, where the rooms are oversized and underfurnished. The dogs are on an airplane overnight, landing in the morning. She worries they won't survive the journey. She takes a sleeping pill that night.

The next day, the customs check takes a few hours, so it is afternoon when the dogs finally reach her. She has set up their bowls and the old stinky cushions that she brought vacuum packed, as well as new dog beds. Both dogs are clean and so are their cages, but perhaps they have been cleaned by the receiving kennel staff. They seem to be in good shape. It is very hot, so they just let the dogs explore the house and garden, offer them some food, and watch them flop in exhaustion on their smelly old cushions, rejecting the new beds.

The house feels less empty now.

She is always considering her dogs' deaths. It is something she thinks about almost every day, looking at them. Imagines that one day they'll be gone. And that more likely than not, she will have to take the decision to kill them, and she will have to watch them die. She thinks about this a lot. The best option would be at home, in their beds, of course. Perhaps she will be spared the actual death, but will find them peacefully 'asleep,' only a little cold and stiff, in the morning when she wakes up. Then, in descending order, she would prefer euthanasia at home, in the dogs' favourite spot, holding their heads in her lap, stroking them tenderly. A death she'd like for herself, saying goodbye at the right time, before indignity and pain. Being gently stroked on the head, hand held, thank you and good bye. Not see you on the other side. No side. Just the end. She feels panic rising and thinks of her dogs again. Is thinking about the dogs' deaths a way not to think of her own? A safe way to think of death, the one moment you know is coming. All other moments are contingent, even taxes can be avoided. This one is not. It will happen. The dogs will die and so will she.

She must continue her list of ever less preferable dog death scenarios. She must face them now, in her head, so she knows she won't break apart then. Except she did break, as the little one was slipping away, she let out a cry and bent over to hold her head tight. One of the few entirely unmediated emotional reactions in her life. It seemed sentimental to her, like a performance of grief, but it was for real. The dog had been ill, but not too long. The decision easy. The saying goodbye – the killing – in the veterinary surgery, but they'd brought the little one's bed. Lying there between them, asking for more pats with her paw. A lump, tears, just thinking about it. She did break. Her first death. It's just a dog. But it is a death. A death that belongs to her. Her death.

Thinking about worse deaths seems perverse, yet she must. A longer, more painful illness, a debilitating old age. Strokes, heart attacks, broken spines or necks, poisonings and snake bites. Inability to save, inability to ease the passage. Watching writhing, hearing screams, gasps. The incomprehension in their eyes, the reflexive bite, the shit and piss of a dying dog. It doesn't bear thinking of, she must think it. Yet, the worst of the worst is the missed death. The accident or fatal illness and inevitable euthanasia when she is not there. Not being able to say goodbye, not being able to witness, to take the responsibility, no, that's not the word, not being able to take part in their death as in their life. Not fulfilling what's been started. Is it about owning a creature, a life, so completely? This imagining of the dogs' death is a fantasy of completion. Is that why she owns dogs instead of having children?

The next evening, they take the dogs for a walk to the end of their road, where there is a small park, and back again. It isn't far but it is still hot and she wants to acclimatise them slowly. They haven't walked down this way before, their house is right at the beginning of the road, near a drag of shops and restaurants, so they haven't needed to. They realise their house, that feels so big, is probably the most modest one on the street. The most popular architectural style in the area is modern and massive, houses that are sleek assemblages of big concrete boxes with glass sides, stacked and juxtaposed against each other, with elements of variation and whimsy, pitched roof, steel details, voids and ornaments. The houses have little garden space, although they often incorporate a swimming pool on a concrete patio, surrounded by stylish potted palms or a row of cacti in gravel. Several houses like this are in the process of being built, successors to an older design, kind of mock colonial with columns and balconies with balustrades and tiled roofs. Some have Chinese green and blue glazed tiles. These houses have a little more space around them, a patch of grass, a fence or even hedge, but nevertheless they dominate the area of land they occupy. Left in between these great beasts are a few even older houses, single storey like theirs. Many are a weather-beaten, and they stand in less manicured plots, some still with big lawns around them with trees and shrubs. Several appear empty, padlocked and dark, waiting to be razed to the ground, and the gardens to be filled with great concrete boxes with glass sides. What a great place to hide a body, they laugh.

In the small park the dogs have a pee against a palm tree and a roll in the grass. It's not much of a park, and the grass is the coarse, stubbly tropical variety, but it's a space away from the pavement. On the way back, less blinded by the architectural foibles of the their street, they count luxury cars. There are five orange Lamborghinis.

When they come back from the dog walk they head out into the sticky night to get some food for themselves. They have dog bowls but no plates, knives or forks. They walk the few metres to the beginning of their road, but rather than stopping at their local bars, they veer right and walk to the next crossing, turning left into a bigger road. Five minutes' walk past some condo complexes brings them to even more restaurants and a mall or two. There are also some very pretty two-storey shophouses, pastel coloured with decorated shutters on the second floor, the lower floor occupied by businesses, fronted by a covered patio connecting to the houses next-door, making a sheltered walkway along the street. Most of the downstairs businesses are restaurants, the choice of cuisine is wide, from local to global, traditional to modern. It is hard to choose. They don't want to be away from the dogs for too long, so they settle for something fast. A chain that serves Bavarian sausages and beer, he has been before. The food is not bad, but somehow doesn't taste quite right. She wonders if it is the ingredients, the preparation or just the atmosphere itself. Things taste differently in different climates; the air changes the tastebuds or maybe the chemistry of the food. Besides, she guesses eating European food in Asia is like Asian food in Europe, similar but a little adapted for the local market. The beer is cold and lovely in the heat.

On the way back they pop into a supermarket at the bottom level of the nearest mall. It is an upmarket chain, carrying all sorts of overpriced Western foods, as well as overpriced local produce. Here you can get European meats and cheeses, rotisserie chicken and sushi in the deli, and the same cereal packets as everywhere else in the world. They discover the place also stocks a number of branded items from their favourite supermarket at home. The best find is coffee. The traditional local coffee scene is dominated by instant, sweet, milky. They later learn that the Asian market is used to drinking the lesser quality robusta beans, since the arabica was always sold, at a higher price, to the West. The global coffee culture is making inroads here too, but most of the home market for espresso-based beverages is dominated by the pod manufacturers and their specific machines. So the grounds and beans available are mostly imported. He finds her favourite kind, the Sumatra Mandheling sold by the shop at home. She is pleased, already she has missed her coffee. She has a look at the packet, is it really the same stuff she got at home? Yes. The coffee has come all the way from a mountainside just around the corner from Singapore, been sent to Berkshire in England, put in bags, and shipped all the way back again.

2. Grind and Chop

She makes coffee every morning. For years after arriving in the United Kingdom she had been a tea drinker. Maybe she had tried to fit in. Then she rediscovered coffee, and it felt like coming home. When she had lived in Italy briefly she'd become addicted to the very strong, very small coffees drunk in one shot standing at the bar of the coffee shop located underneath the language school at which she taught. Like a true addict she would feel the urge for a *caffe*, drinking it sweet, black, and quick, she could feel it enter her bloodstream, spreading a delicious vigour though her veins.

These days she prefers her coffee long and plentiful. The making of it is a kind of ritual. She has a simple but trusted filter coffee machine, like the one her father has always used. The first step is to empty the old grounds from the filter, left from the previous morning; she knocks the filter out against the edge of the metal bin, one, two, three. Always three times. Then, she washes the filter out under the tap and places it back into the cradle of the coffee machine, rinses the glass jug under the tap, swirling it a few times, fills the jug to the four-cup marker and pours the water into the tank of the coffee brewer, opening and shutting its black plastic lid.

She gets some coffee beans out of the freezer, takes the clothes peg off the folded top of the bag of coffee beans, opens it, puts it to her nose, and smells the beans. They don't smell of much. She puts some beans into the grinder, folds the top of the bag, replaces the clothes peg, and returns the bag to the freezer. She has a long look at the intact beans in the grinder. Their dark brown colour, their sheen, the little S-shaped groove in the middle. She wonders how many beans are in the grinder as she places the transparent plastic lid on it and presses the button on the front of the machine starting the grinding with a loud whirr.

The beans are instantly crushed. She will never find out how many beans there were in the grinder. It will remain a mystery. Nobody will ever possess that information and yet it existed, it was a part of the great, colossally complex equation that makes up the universe. She remembers how as a child, when she still believed in the afterlife but had rejected the naïve picture of heaven painted by the nuns in her school, she had thought that when one died one would finally know everything. That was what death or heaven or everlasting life was: getting all the answers, finding out how the universe worked, what the meaning of life was, how many coffee beans there had been in the grinder that morning. Everything would be revealed. There would be no more confusion, or darkness, or sin.

She releases the button and the machine stops grinding. She pulses a few times for good measure and turns the grinder upside down to collect the grounds in the lid. Now the fragrance of the coffee has been released she savours it for a little while. First removing the measuring spoon from the empty tin, she puts the ground coffee into a container, then measures out four spoons into the filter, and swings the cradle closed, securing it with a piece of Sellotape stuck to the side of the machine. The catch broke a long time ago. She presses the on button and the orange light goes on. She doesn't believe in everlasting life anymore; she will die without knowing how many coffee beans there had been in the grinder.

Some evenings she tries to cook. The kitchen is built for a household with a live-in maid. It is impractical and badly designed in terms of ease of use and efficiency – in the European manner. She feels like she has to walk twice as much as in her kitchen in London whenever she prepares food. The cupboards, sleek and modern to look at, are awkward to open, banging annoyingly against each other. This kitchen is divided into a dry kitchen and a wet kitchen, a concept entirely new to her. The dry kitchen is large with an island and without any appliances save a built-in oven. This must be a concession to possible Western tenants, as Chinese households tend not to use ovens. 'This is where you make your cocktails and entertain your guests,' her husband had explained the dry kitchen in a video he made for her before she arrived. The wet kitchen is small and cramped with a gas cooker and a sink and a fridge and not really any worktop space at all, and no air conditioning. It connects to the small space at the back with a tiny bathroom that is meant to be the maid's quarters. No aircon here either, only slatted windows that could never be closed but would admit any breeze there may be so whenever it was be breezy the maid wouldn't miss the breeze. But they don't have a maid, and cooking in the wet kitchen is hot and bothersome and anti-social. All the preparation has to be done in the dry kitchen cool – where was the maid meant to do it? – and then she has to walk over, through the door to the stove, and the heat, and do the cooking, struggling to find space for all the dishes of chopped and sliced or marinated and mixed ingredients. She starts cooking more things that can be done solely in an oven.

She turns the oven on, sets it to 180 degrees Celsius, and takes a roasting tin out of a drawer and some olive oil from the cupboard. The door creaks irritatingly, and no amount of oiling has helped: the door is hung badly. She puts enough olive oil in the roasting tin to cover its bottom and puts it in the oven to heat up. Going to the wet kitchen she picks up a chopping board drying on the rack over the sink, takes it to the island in the dry kitchen, and then goes back to the wet kitchen and takes courgettes, carrots, and peppers out of the fridge. She returns to the cupboard in the dry kitchen and opens it again – another creak – and gets onion and garlic. 'Call You and Yours' is on Radio 4, which has been playing in the kitchen all day. 'In Touch' used to be on when she started cooking, but now she has moved seven time zones away it is the British public's chance to have their say on the consumer issue highlighted by the parent programme. Neither 'In Touch' or 'Call You and Yours' is something she would go out of her way to listen to. Information for blind people, or discussions about pensions, or getting your kids into school, or cycling lanes. It doesn't really matter, she likes listening to most things on Radio 4, she finds she learns something almost every time she listens. How much of this information she retains, she has no idea. She turns it off when the

Archers come on.

Now they are discussing food and mental health on 'Call You and Yours' and she chops an onion roughly. She slices the garlic. Cooking is good for your mental health. The courgette she halves and then slices into half-moons. She treats the carrot the same. Doing something with your hands. She slices the top and the bottom off the green pepper and cuts the middle open and deseeds it by sliding the knife along its inside, severing each membrane attaching the seed pod in the middle to the walls of the outside of the pepper. Something creative. Removing the stalk, she cuts the flesh into pieces a square centimetre in size. She does the same to a red pepper. Turning produce into deliciousness. She places all these chopped and sliced vegetables on a plate. Once the oven is hot, she takes the roasting tin out and tips the vegetables into the hot oil. It sizzles and spits. She stirs the vegetable pieces with a wooden spoon to cover them with oil, then returns the tin to the oven. Food is a way to connect with people. She sets the timer for fifteen minutes, after which she stirs the vegetables again. They are going a little wrinkly and soft. Eating together as a family is important. Fifteen minutes later they are browning at the edges and she agitates them again, and adds a tin of chopped tomatoes, a couple of tablespoons of tomato paste, some herbs, salt and pepper, a dash of soy sauce, and one of tabasco and a pinch of sugar, before stirring again and returning to the oven. Finding joy in the everyday. A simple roast vegetable sauce for pasta or gnocchi. A vegetarian favourite. She finds cooking so utterly tedious. She boils the kettle for pasta water.

He returns from work. Having spent the day in air conditioning and taken the cool bus home, he still somehow looks fresh in khaki chinos and a shirt, open at the neck, no tie. Looks relaxed, but tired. He has his earphones in as he walks through the door, perhaps he has taken a call on the bus, or perhaps he is listening to music, she doesn't know. He takes them out and says hello and stands by the kitchen island looking through the post. He is in his socks, they heed the Asian style of the house, and take their shoes off at the door. There are low shoe cupboards on the sides of on the large entrance porch, making two benches on which one can sit to take footwear on and off. But because they just slip what's on their feet off at the door, shoes are accumulating and taking over the porch space, like an uneven rug of footwear. Even in his socks he stands much taller than her, a whole head's height. She likes his height, and the way he carries it. His posture is one of the things that attracted her to him, still does. Always a straight back, she but it reminds her of her own slouch. She straightens a bit, instinctively.

They have pasta and roast vegetable sauce, with pre-grated parmesan on top, which she hates the idea of but actually quite likes. It is salty and brings out the taste of the sauce, does the job a sprinkling of parmesan on your pasta is meant to do. They have a glass of red wine and watch an episode of some crime drama or other on the TV, via the internet and a setup that fools the website into thinking that they are in the right country for the content they want to watch. They never watch live TV anymore; the set has not been plugged into an aerial for years. She kind of misses it, the connection that live TV gave you, the feeling that you were part of something with all these people that were watching together at the same time. The next day everyone talked about the latest episode, the cliff-hanger. Whole nations came together to speculate on who did it. Now you have to be careful of spoilers. That's why networks release their online content at specific times, to create a buzz. People like it that way, need the community. Social media has replaced live TV in that respect, she thinks. As a source of news, as a place to connect, to make communities. The boundaries may have shifted somewhat, but the effect is the same. The gathering around the fireside to tell stories. To read books. To listen to the radio. To watch TV. To check Twitter. She is sad the TV pushed out the fire, she likes fires. But here it is too hot anyway.

At first it seems like fun. A holiday setting, taking your dogs to the beach. Walking in warm waves on golden sand. At first, she enjoys it. Despite the container ships on the horizon, despite the motorway bordering the beach park, despite the debris the sea throws up on the shore. They do clean it away very quickly, teams of litter pickers descending on the beach just after dawn, but she is usually even earlier than them. She has to be. It is so incredibly hot she soon starts dreading dog walks. She isn't a morning person, but they have to be out of the house by daybreak to stand a chance of a semi-decent walk. Daybreak is always around seven am. By eight in the morning, it is already so hot she starts worrying about the dogs' welfare. For morning walks she drives to a few places where she can sneak them off the lead, hoping they'll have a bit of exercise. First thing, in the flush of morning excitement and before the heat has bitten, they manage some runs, a few chases and gambols, but soon they are so warm they slow down, tongues lolling, and they follow her at a slow lope. Evenings are even worse, they wait until the last hour of daylight, because the girl does not like to walk in the dark, and take a turn in the neighbourhood. They all relish coming back home into the air conditioning. The dogs drink, she drinks, they all flop, cooling down. She is already dreading the morning walk of the next day. Walks used to be her moments of presence, of peace, a time to recharge, reset thoughts, breathe deeply and feel oneself in the now. A kind of meditation. A dog walk makes everything better, she used to think. Now they are just chores. She has a stomach ache thinking about all the walks in the heat she will have to do in Singapore. Two every day. Day in and day out. She has to go to the toilet.

3. Laura

Laura sits in front of the piano again. It is a small apartment, but she has found this space in the passage between the kitchen and living room, where the Yamaha fits perfectly. Since they moved to Singapore, she has the time and just enough space to do all the things she never had time to do when she ran the salon. Other expats, especially the wives, always ask her why she doesn't set up a hair place here. She'd get so many customers, cutting western hair, the local hairdressers just can't do it right. But this was meant to be a new start, an adventure, she doesn't want to do what she's always done, she wants to use the time, the money, learning something new. Not that the money goes that far, it seemed a lot before they got out here and realised how much rent was. And the car. And supermarket prices. Wine. Washing up liquid. The brand of cereal that she liked. She can't find anything similar here. Tom brings back bags of stuff from home whenever he travels for work, it is so much cheaper that way. Everyone seems to be able to splash the cash here, but she is always worried. She can't buy a piano but she is renting one, giving herself the time to learn, finally.

She always wanted to play the piano. Now it is here in the hallway she sits in front of it every day without fail. In the beginning she played for hours. The simple scales that the teacher had given her, a little ditty or two. Chopsticks. Today she sits by the piano, the lid open and her hands on the keys, just as she has become practiced at placing them. She hasn't made a sound for half an hour. She stares out of the living room balcony doors, which she can see part of from her place in the hallway if she turns he head a little, leans back just a tiny bit. They are on the eleventh floor and through the doors she can see the sky and the tops of other building in the distance. There are grey clouds and there is grey concrete. Their apartment looks out over the marina; on National Day the sky is lit up by fireworks and they have front row seats. It seems like she has been sitting here by the piano and stared at the empty sky every day for as long as she can remember.

Laura stopped the tuition a couple of years ago, it was too expensive, but she refuses to get rid of the piano. Its super shiny surface doesn't gather dust because she wipes it at least three times a week. The flat is small and easy to clean, it doesn't take her long and she can't stand things not being clean and tidy. She does a little bit of cleaning every day during the week and without her really trying the place stays spotless. Tom being home over the weekend messes it up, and she doesn't want to clean when he is around, so on Monday morning after she has dropped him off at work in the car, she relishes coming home and tidying and cleaning and washing. She is usually done by midday.

She allows herself one lunch out each week. Everyone else seems to be constantly out, lunching, shopping, yogaing. How can they afford it? They all have maids too, but that isn't the expensive bit. The wine they consume each week easily costs more than they pay the maid. Their damn personal trainers, to help them work off those extra calories. She has a bike and takes long rides along the East Coast Park, all the way to the airport and back. She walks the dog. She practices the piano. Except recently, not so much, not for some time now.

As she stares out at the sky she wonders if she is depressed. She doesn't feel depressed. She feels like she always felt, like she has felt for the past five years here in Singapore. Nothing much at all. She still isn't sure she likes it here, but she doesn't hate it, either. Maybe she should read more, she thinks, but if she is being honest, she isn't much into books. She reads the occasional bestseller, usually on holiday, because that's what one does on holiday. It isn't that she doesn't enjoy reading, she does, but it seems so. Unproductive. You start a book, you read it, and at the end you are left with a read book, spent. She likes doing things practical things. Cutting hair, dusting surfaces. She wants to do something with results. Like learning to play the piano.

4. Frying Salt

They meet on an evening walk to the local dog exercise area. There are designated dog runs in many parks, although she soon realises her dogs find these only moderately interesting. The runs are too small, and there are often other dogs in there. Her dogs like large empty spaces, like the beach where they go almost every morning. Dog parks don't tend to be particularly pleasant for humans either, although in Singapore poops are fastidiously picked. But she's heard reports of tick infestation, and there are certainly mosquitos that bite her legs, so altogether it is an unappealing destination. But there are not that many destinations to choose from, so occasionally she goes there. It is, at least, in a shaded park, so a little cooler than the sun-beat streets.

Laura and Tom are walking as a couple, with their small dog. They are British and she feels she comes over as desperate to talk to them. She is desperate. The ritual chats of her London dog walks are becoming a distant memory. Singaporean dog owners seem uninterested in talking, and downright scared of letting the dogs meet. Crossing to the other side of the road is a common reaction by any other dog walker on seeing her and the dogs. Perhaps it is the size of them. Perhaps it is her. White expats are far more likely to stop, let the dogs sniff each other and talk. Chinese Singaporeans very occasionally, Indian Singaporeans more so, and Malays do not have dogs.

She has not spoken to many people in Singapore yet, and the sense of isolation is creeping in and, although she was ready for it, thought she'd cope with it well, maybe even like it, it scares her. Here an opportunity presents itself, people in the same position as her in this alien world, with a ready-made opening. They talk about the dogs and then, although she feels a bit forward, she suggests getting together, dog walks, maybe drinks, exchanges numbers. She knows she's the new girl in town, looking for friends, but they have mentioned a park nearby she hasn't discovered yet, where apparently you can take your dogs off lead without much trouble. If nothing else, she needs that park. She needs more space. The beach is becoming boring. A good green space for the dogs and her to roam is what she wants. A proper dog walk. A place to feel free.

Tom works for the same bank as her husband. Laura doesn't work. Inevitably Laura and she meet far more often than they do all together. Laura shows her the Gardens by the Bay East, the little sister of the showpiece Gardens by the Bay. They have already driven in that direction once after being told of a good space for dogs, but stopped too early, just after the waterfront condos over the river from the stadium. There is a large meadow there, where the maids take the dogs down from the apartments. Had they continued further, turning left towards the golf course under the expressway bridge, but instead of going into the course, keep on straight, they would have reached the gardens located on the Eastern side of Marina Bay. The large coolhouse and dryhouse domes of the main gardens are visible across the water, and the supertrees behind, the Marina Bay Sands towering above them, and on the other side of the mouth of the river the wheel of the Singapore flyer, and the backdrop of the central business district. It is an impressive view, gorgeous in the evening when the glittering lights of the city take over from the last gleam of the setting sun on skyscraper glass.

The park itself is an elongated series of lawns, bordered by trees and shrubs, ponds andbioswales – drainage courses that fill up with water and croaking frogs during rainy season. It isn't huge, but it is usually empty, and the few dog walkers there seem to have a tacit agreement to let their dogs run free. The dogs like it more than the plain sand of the beach. It is very quiet too, except for weekends, when it always seems to be the start or finish of some fun run or race, hordes of people in identical T-shirts sweating it around the paths of the park and across the barrage. The park is well manicured, with garden workers continually busy with some task of upkeep or other. It is situated on relatively recently reclaimed land, they learn, along with the golf course bordering it. After land is reclaimed it needs to settle for a decade or two before any major buildings can be erected. The land in the Gardens by the Bay East is still settling, often the drainage courses overflow, trees fall over as their roots are unable to hold on to waterlogged earth. Although the garden workers are wary of her dogs, she is happy to have them around. The more human activity in the bushes the less snakes in the undergrowth, she thinks.

She has realised there are snakes in Singapore. Serious snakes, like king cobras and six-foot pythons. There are anecdotes of dogs being bitten. She thought her large dogs safe, but of course not, pythons prey on deer and such; she has read of a thirty-kilo dog being attacked by a python in Hong Kong. She knows that snakes are shy, and unlikely to be aggressive, but nonetheless she worries about accidents. Most of the beach is open sand, but in areas whey they have to walk through undergrowth, she goes in front of the dogs and stomps her feet to scare any serpents away. In Gardens by The Bay East the biggest danger to the dogs seems to be the enormous monitor lizards that occasionally appear near the ponds on cooler days, warming themselves in the morning sun. The dogs are interested, although a little wary. The lizards, despite their fearsome appearance, tend to slip away into the water at any approach. One, which makes it a little further away from a pond, is courted by the girl in a combination of play bows and cautious attacks, and yet it doesn't strike. She quickly leashes the dog, she doesn't want to test the lizard's patience. Monitor lizards have big teeth, and their infamy for being poisonous, she's read, is due to them harbouring such a potent flora of bacteria in their mouths that their prey, once bitten, dies of sepsis even if it getsaway, and is later sought out and devoured.

Not long after they arrive, in some sort of orientation day, they are taken by the relocation agent to a local wet market and a supermarket, to show them the options of where to shop in their new neighbourhood. It feels like sightseeing. The wares on offer are colourful and exotic, many entirely unknown to her. Fruit and greens, all kinds of seafood and then prepared stuff like fresh tofu and fishballs and dried things she has no idea what they could be. Prices are rarely displayed, and she wouldn't know what would be a fair price even for the items she recognises. The agent says it is cheaper than the supermarket, and she does not doubt that, the supermarket is expensive. The supermarket is much more western, with labels, prices, packaging. Not wet – dry and contained. But she is keen on the new experience, of making herself at home. She can cook pasta and sauce forever, buying incredibly overpriced imported ingredients – tinned tomatoes are a rarity, hidden on shelves, priced in multiples of what they go for at home. Or, she thinks, she could learn how to cook with local stuff. Learn to recognise all the fantastic goods on display in the wet market, know their price and use, shop like a local. She decides she should take cooking lessons.

Laura has lived in Singapore for some years, but every time her husband goes back home for a business trip, or any family visit, they come laden with at least a suitcase full of items – everything from chocolate to dishwasher liquid. Even the global versions of the same brand do not deliver the same quality as the home bought stuff, according to Laura. Nevertheless, Laura is happy to join for an afternoon of cooking instruction. It is something to do, perhaps.

She picks Laura up in her car. The cooking class takes place in a residential house a short drive from where they live. The teaching kitchen is out the back of a bungalow, four cooking stations under an awning, cooled only by fans. It gets hot. The classes are run by a stern middle-aged Indian-Singaporean woman, assisted by her helper, who prepares trays of ingredients, cleans up, and is held up both as an example – 'Here is some I prepared earlier, look how finely Emma has chopped the ginger, this is what you are aiming for – finely, finely' – and as a problem – 'I told her not to disturb me with phone calls during class, she is new, it is so difficult to train staff these days.'

They make silken tofu with herbs, Sichuan chicken with cashew nuts, stir fried kai-lan. She finally learns of one Chinese vegetable, and how to cook it the way it is served in restaurants and hawker centres. She realises the key to Chinese recipes is the mixing together in right quantities of many condiments: dark soy, light soy, Shaoxing wine, rice vinegar, oyster sauce, sesame oil. Fried ginger and garlic and spring onions add to the flavour mix. As long as you know what and how much, it's not too hard. But remembering that is not easy, she keeps the printed paper recipes she's given at this class, they become crumpled and stained with use as she always needs to refer to the specific mix of sauces for any given dish, otherwise the taste is just not the same. Similar but not quite the same, like the local Nestle and Kraft and Unilever products Laura finds lacking.

The woman shows them her favourite brands of condiments, tells them where they can be found (in the supermarket, their exotic appearance to foreigners belying their ubiquity). She dutifully takes photos of the bottles as aide-memoirs.

They get split into pairs – there are two sets of friends and one loner forming a group of her own with help from the maid – and given trays of ingredients for each dish in turn. They get shown how to chop ginger, along the fibres (or was it across, she honestly cannot remember), how to chop spring onions, one method for the white part and another for the green, they mix sauces into little bowls, measuring a spoonful of this and a pinch of that. When the ingredients are prepared, they use large woks to cook. She learns that the secret to Chinese stir frying is to fry a pinch of salt in the pan first, releasing its flavours, before adding the oil. The oil is hot enough when it bubbles around a wooden spoon dipped in it. Some recipes call for ginger, sometimes garlic, to be quickly fried first and the crispy slices or fronds fished out for later use. The oil becomes flavoured. The correct stir-frying technique is athletic, they are told, and the teacher shouts at them to work harder, stir more vigorously.

The Sichuan chicken calls for more dried chili peppers than chicken. They are told they can reduce the number for a milder version. They all do, but it is still almost unbearably hot when they come to eat it. After they have cooked their dishes, the maid sets a table on the veranda at the front of the house, and they sit down to eat the fruits of their labour. The flavours are not what she expected. Perhaps they are more authentically Chinese. The silken tofu is too gelatinous and its sauce is too herby, the chicken too spicy. The kai-lan, fried in garlic and a mix of oyster and other sauces and a touch of fresh chili, is the most palatable to her. This she will make again and again. But she will always remember the frying of the salt too late, when she has already added the oil to a cold pan the way she has always done.

There are, unsurprisingly, six white women around the table. The conversation inevitably moves to living in Singapore as an expat. She is the newest arrival, gets quizzed on how she is finding it. Her first statement, question, is always about the heat.

'The heat! How do you live with this heat? Does it ever stop?' No. It does not. Some say you get used to it.

'When I first came here I looked at the locals wearing trousers and thought how is that possible? But see I am wearing jeans today. It's fine,' one woman says.

Others look more uncomfortable.

'We try to use the air conditioning as little as possible, otherwise you never get used to the heat,' says another.

She marvels at both statements. She cannot imagine wearing long jeans or turning off the constant flow of cool air in her house. Sleeping in the heat is surely impossible. If you keep going in and out of the cold your body never adjusts, one of the women continues. She wonders how you canpossibly avoid doing that in Singapore, with its offices and malls and coffee shops and cinemas all chilled to arctic temperatures. Maybe the woman does not get out much? Does she work, she asks, but no, she has kids. They all have kids except Laura and she, who have dogs. She thinks, what about the poor husband, he works in an air conditioned office no doubt, how is he to adjust? but she doesn't say anything.

The conversation somehow moves to maids. She learns that from the mention of work or kids it is not far to the mention of maids.

'I'm looking for a cleaner, can anybody recommend anyone?' she asks. Turns out they can't.

'Why a cleaner, why not a maid?' asks one of the women, the one there alone. She replies she doesn't want a maid and, apart from the fact that there just isn't enough for a maid to do as it is just her and her husband and her dogs, she'd feel uncomfortable. The loner says getting a helper is the best thing she's ever done, she has two kids of course, but even without, they're just such a... help. And the discomfort, minimal, you get used to it, really. Laura does not have a maid, nor a cleaner. They do live in a small flat, and Laura, to be fair, does not seem to do much – she doesn't work, and has no plans to either, despite professing boredom. But to Laura it is a matter of pride, it seems, to do the housework. Her husband works, she runs the house. To her surprise the other pair of friends concur. They have kids, and no maids. No, they do everything themselves.

'I came here to support my husband, so that's what I do, take care of the kids, of the house, cook.'

Maybe that's why this woman is in the heat all the time, she thinks, baffled, but surely, she must air condition the car? But she stays quiet now as they discuss domestic chores and domestic help. She tries another bite of the chicken, it really is ridiculously hot, so she reaches for the water. She doesn't want someone living in her house, but she doesn't want to clean either. Supporting her husband? She walks the dogs, and cooks, but she doesn't do it just for him, the dogs are theirs together, and she has to eat, too, and she is planning on getting some kind of work, to teach again, and to read and write and do her own things, the things make her*her*.

The conversation fizzles out, the class and lunch are over and they all go their separate ways. She gives Laura a lift back to her flat, not far from their house. She thinks maybe they should have gone for a flat? The house is so big, everyone expects her to have a maid, how is she going to clean it? Lots of people have dogs in flats here. But the thought of having to take the dogs in the lift every day... No the house is definitely better. Laura has been over to theirs for coffee, and a snoop no doubt. Asked about the rent, which is exorbitant, but complimented the house, the nicest she's seen. She couldn't but feel some pride. But no pool sadly, no. The maid's room, though, pronounced Laura, is positively luxurious. People in their condo have their maids sleep in the bomb shelters, which are nothing but fortified box rooms. Yes, Laura explained, they go buy toddler's cots from IKEA, the maids are all so small, and a fan perhaps. This has windows, Laura looked the room over, and its own bathroom.

'I would get a maid if I had this room,' Laura had said, 'I'd get her just to look after the dog when we go away.'

5. Cut

She returns from her walk with the dogs, and after allowing enough time for everyone to cool down, she feeds them. The old boy is a fussy eater with a sensitive stomach, and she is always trying to buy things that will excite his palate and make him eat. She finds frozen liver, lung and tripe in a large supermarket. She defrosts the vacuum-packed innards, and she cuts the bags open, careful not to spill the liquid inside. Preparing food for her dogs is something she enjoys.

She starts with the liver. She pours the dark red blood into a Tupperware container and places a piece on the chopping board. She takes a kitchen knife out of the rack and the sharpener out of a drawer and sharpens the knife passing it, heel to tip, over two steel rods in the plastic casing of the sharpener. She starts with the piece of liver, a rough oval in shape. She cuts a couple of one-centimetre slices off the side, then chops these into small squares, which she places in the plastic container with the blood. The liver is dark and silky and cuts easily, oozing a little liquid. It smells like steel. There's something about cutting meat that is just more interesting than chopping vegetables. When she is done with the liver, she cuts open the packet of beef lung. There is less liquid in it, and it's a watery pink. She is fascinated by these things that once were alive. She places the lung, a similar shape and size to the initial piece of liver but thicker, on the chopping board. Again, she slices it first, then chops. But the lung is not so easy to cut, it is uneven in texture, spongey, with membranes and crunchy bronchioles growing through it. She thinks about the animal to which this lung once belonged: it lived by this ingenious organ, inspiring air into those crunchy tubes, the strange foamy flesh extracting oxygen, releasing carbon dioxide, and expelling it through the tubules. Now it is dead meat. She has to saw and hack at the pieces. She needs a butcher's knife.

Finally, she gets to the tripe. She is a little apprehensive. It has none of the beauty of the liver, or the anatomical fascination of the lung.

There is little liquid coming out of its packet, it retains all its juices in its own permeable, shaggy moistness. It unfolds into sheets, one side darker, thickly furred, the other, light in colour, muscular and bare. It smells. She tries to think of the fascinating absorption of nutrients through this ungainly blanket of flesh, but it only makes her revulsion worse. The organ responsible for turning food into shit. Disembowelling must be a wretched affair, why the Japanese would choose to make it a matter of honour she cannot fathom. The ritual whereby the kaishakunin beheads the suicidee at the mere reach for their knife, rather than after the cut in the abdomen is made, has nothing to do with lessening pain, she realises, it is to prevent the stench, the grotesque spilling of guts filled with excrement, into the fine ceremonial halls of Japan. Harakiri on the battlefield, which stinks of blood and mud and dead mens' piss is one thing. Seppukku in front of an audience, quite another.

She mixes the pieces of liver, lung and tripe in the Tupperware container with her hands. The pieces feel cold and slimy, some a little rougher. Her hand comes up pinkish wet, and she rinses it under the tap. She puts the Tupperware container in the microwave, one minute on high, to just cook the pieces of innards. While the microwave hums away, she gets the large metal dog bowls, and adds a scoop of kibble to each. Three loud beeps. She opens the microwave oven hatch and stirs the pieces in the container with a fork. She closes the door and sets the oven for another minute on high. She gets the faintest whiff of cooked liver and it immediately brings back memories of torturous school meals. She has never been able to eat liver, even though she's told sautéed liver, chicken or calf, can be very nice indeed. When she was a pupil at the convent school, liver was served in overcooked slabs in grey-brown gravy, with boiled potatoes. It was the meal she dreaded the most, she could smell it the very moment she entered school in the morning. There was no escaping lunch, pupils had to eat what they were given, gratefully. Once you finished your meal you were allowed out to play for the rest of the lunch hour. She'd be stuck on her own in the dining hall, staring at her plate, trying to swallow down pieces of liver. As she got older, she started spitting mouthfuls into a napkin, hiding it in her pocket and flushing it down the toilet. But she always remembers, still bristles at it thirty years later, being told to think of the poor starving children in Ethiopia. What a nonsensical thing to tell a child, which with its child's clear logic cannot see what earthly difference it will make to those emaciated forms that she has seen on TV (they scared her a lot) whether she eats this slab of liver or not. She repeatedly fantasised about stuffing the liver, gravy and potato and all, into a jiffy bag marked 'Starving Children, Ethiopia, Africa, The World,' and shoving it into a post-box, stained and leaking, in front of the teacher, the sanctimonious nun. 'There! There you go, I am thinking of the starving children, are you happy now?!'

She takes the part-cooked liver and lung and tripe and mixes some with the kibble in each bowl. She adds a little water to cool the pieces down and to mix some of the liver and lung and tripe juices with the dry kibble. The dogs are around, but they know not to beg. The girl is lying in the corner of the kitchen and observing her keenly, and the old boy has stuck his head around the corner of the door from the master bedroom a few times, then disappeared off again. She calls him now, and the girl gets up, keen. The old boy appears at the doorway, and she tells them to wait. She never lets her dogs throw themselves at their food. They must wait until she gives them the sign. She puts the bowls in their stands. 'Go on then!' It is the signal that they can approach, and both the dogs do so and eat the innards with relish.

6. Mr Lee Liat Heng

He sits in the little office at the back of the body shop and looks at his fish. There are no windows in the room except for a small oblong up near the ceiling, so soiled that only the murkiest light filters through it. There is glass in the door, but the door leads only to the gloom of the garage. His desk is lit up by an anglepoise lamp, its yellow light glaring back at him from the sheets of paper strewn in front of him. He takes off his reading glasses and rubs the bridge of his nose. With a sigh he opens the top drawer of a filing cabinet behind him and takes out a small tub of flaked fish food.

The room contains nothing but the desk, two chairs, several filing cabinets, and the fish tanks, but manoeuvring between them is tricky even for a small man like him. Some of the fish tanks, placed on top of a filing cabinet standing on top of another filing cabinet, require him to take them down and set them on the desk before he can reach to sprinkle the flakes in the water. He carefully moves one tank at a time, feeding the fish a pinch each, then replaces them before moving on to the next container. There are at least a dozen plastic tanks around the room, each with one or two partitions, separating the solitary territories of two or three fish. Some fish are monochrome, bright orange or electric blue, a few almost black, others intensely red. One is entirely white. Some display two colours on the extensive trains of their fins. Red tips on blue bodies or sinister black edges, slashes of orange and streaks of pink. A few show variations of three hues, an almost unbelievable combination of pattern, colour, folds and fronds. To most of them there is more fin than fish. Their tails are like the banners of armies fluttering in the breeze, different constellations of colours signalling allegiances to different lords.

The partitions of the tanks can be removed, lifted out, allowing the fish to meet, but he rarely lets that happen. If he had to choose, he would never lift the partitions, never break the fragile peace between the proud aquatic armies in his care. But every now and again he is persuaded to so that his employers can place bets, watching the colourful creatures in his care wage an impossible war against each other, for territory they are forced to dispute. Do they believe, he wonders, that they could be kings of double the space they have become accustomed to living in? Do they fight for the sudden possibility of more freedom? He hopes not, because both winner and loser are returned to their halves, or thirds, there is no new kingdom for the victor at the end of the fight. He doesn't like to watch them fight, not because of injuries inflicted, but because of the false promise that he is forced to make to his fish when he lifts those partitions, the sadness he feels putting them back again, when the loser has retreated, money has changed hands, and the gamblers have lost interest. It's good for business, letting his employers have their fun, get excited about the fish, get their money out. They tend to spend more whether they have lost or won, as if the betting is a limbering up exercise, loosening not their muscles but their purses. He doesn't really like working for his employers, but he does anyway.

He repairs cars, that is what he is good at, making the broken whole again, bringing what seemed dead back to life again, improving and making it last. There is little call for that these days, very few people renew the initial certificate of entitlement to own a car for ten years. There are no old cars anymore, no real need for his skills. The cars now on the streets simply need plugging into a computer and, bar accidents, only minor tune-ups. That's why accidents are his main business today, no longer making run but making pretty. Bumps and scrapes smoothed out and polished over, anything more serious usually ends up on the scrapheap or in Malaysia. But there are bumps and scrapes aplenty, and often they need to be made invisible both in reality and on paper. Other times the paper trace needs to be made bigger, bolder than the actual scuff, a few extra dollars, taken not from anyone in particular, but from the insurance companies, everyone knows they cheat us all anyway.

He has kept betta all his life, as did his father. Not for the fighting but for their staggering beauty, the evolutionary signal of strength. Beauty rarely lies, the body conserves resources, and if a body has energy left over for gaudiness and frills, it most likely has enough for brawn. The biggest and brightest fish usually win the fights, but not always. And people love betting for the underdog. Not from a sense of empathy or hope, but for the odds, the chance of a too-good-to-be-true pay-out. It usually is too-good-to-be-true, the underdog retreats, gets shut into his cell until it's time to lose again. He has koi carp in a pond out the back too, and other aquaria inside the garage with the usual cichlids and minnows and goldfish and guppies, but he only keeps bettas in his office.

I am my fish, he thinks: lured by the false promises of escaping this office, baited not by space but by money, more money, more than I could make in a day, in a week, even in a month. But in the end it is never enough, the cut is always smaller, the next job always bigger, just another deal and he'll be let in on more, even double, but it never happens, he is always left with his fraction, it's not even half or a third like the fish get. One more deal he thinks, and I am out, yet still I'm here in my own aquarium, surrounded by fish that never win or lose anything, but keep on fighting.

7. Following Distance

Driving back from a morning walk on the beach, the dogs hot and panting in the back of the leased Honda Jazz. Honda Fit, it is called here. Same car, different name. The steering wheel is on the right side. The back seats are folded down to make room for the hounds, she can see them flopped and panting on the cushions just behind her. Hot and sweaty herself, she is keen to get home into the aircon and make a pot of coffee, maybe read a book. Recover a little before she needs to go out to the shops, into the heat again.

As she turns left into their street, a father and his daughter are crossing, and she slows down. Perhaps a little suddenly because she has not seen them around the corner, but the traffic is thick and nothing happens at any speed. She is surprised to hear a horn just as she feels the car being knocked into. Whoever has hit her has had enough time to beep their horn but not to step on the brake. She sighs inwardly as she stops the car at the curb and puts the hazard lights on. She knows she has the law on her side. The vehicle that has bumped into her is one of those small lorries that look like mini pick-up trucks with canopies over the back, full of construction workers being driven to their site. The driver is a young Chinese Singaporean. He starts arguing as soon as he sees her approaching. She says nothing at first, inspecting the damage: hardly anything, a tiny scratch in the polish on her hatchback. If it was her car she'd let it go, not worth bothering about. But since she is leasing it and she knows the company will charge her for any damage, she has to report it. It's a bother she doesn't want or need, but who knows how much they'll charge, she doesn't want to take the chance of being stung with an extortionate trumped up bill. The young man is telling her it was her fault for stopping suddenly, in the wrong lane. She starts to argue, there were pedestrians, the left lane is blocked by parked cars, but then she stops.

She doesn't have the time or energy for this.

'You drove into the back of me. Please can I have your name and number.' She is already writing down his registration number. The man tries to argue again, but she simply cuts him off, repeating her statement and request. 'You drove into the back of me. Give me your name and number.' He writes down his details on a bit of paper and hands them over, somewhat to her surprise, while he is still trying to make his case. She thanks him.

'I'll be in touch with the leasing company, they will contact you,' she says and walks back to her car. When she gets to her drive, only about twenty metres along the road, she parks and takes some photos of the damage. She sends an email including pictures and the other driver's details to the leasing company and thinks little more of it.

For some reason she thought the matter would simply be noted by the leasing company, it did not occur to her that they would want to see the car or carry out repairs while she is still leasing the vehicle. As to culpability, surely it is a clear case. The highway code states blame for a rear end shunt lies with the colliding vehicle: a safe distance should be kept at all times to the vehicle in front. She assumes the Singaporean highway code, as with so many things in the country, like the three pin electrical plug sockets, closely follows its colonial model. To make sure, she finds the relevant paragraph of the Singaporean Highway code online. The picture attached makes it look like it has been copied from a 1950s English rulebook.

Following Distances

67. To be able to adjust your speed so that you can stop within the space between you and the vehicle in front, you must allow at least one car length for every 16 km/h of your speed.

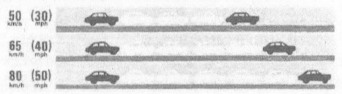

They were moving at much less than 50km/h; she wonders what the speed could have been. Not more than ten kilometres per hour, probably less. Who can work out what the correct following distance is in slow moving traffic, and keep it? She almost feels sorry for the driver that hit her, it is easy to lose concentration momentarily in the morning, in thick, treacly traffic. Then she remembers he seemed to have time enough to hit the horn, but not the brake. What had he expected she'd do? Speed up into the pedestrians? The whole thing was an unfortunate event, but the law is the law, and she is relieved it wasn't the other way around. She expects the matter to be dealt with swiftly and easily. The driver was clearly at work, his company will claim on their insurance and that will be that.

But he does not take the blame. It seems incomprehensible and an utter waste of everyone's time. Perhaps his company will not take the fall, perhaps he'll have to pay himself, or get sanctioned in some way, and it is worth the fight, perhaps admitting culpability would imply some Asian loss of face she doesn't understand.

When the leasing company contacts her to say she must come to their offices with the car, she's reluctant. They need to inspect the damage, they say, take some photos and fill in some forms. It will take no more than ten minutes, they say. Sounds easy enough, so she agrees to come that afternoon, in non-peak hour traffic it should take her no more than thirty minutes.

As she sets off the storm clouds are gathering, and within moments the rain comes down. It is the heaviest rain she has seen in Singapore yet, an incredible tropical downpour, turning the streets twilight dark, except for the frequent flashes of lightning. The thunder comes in immediate claps followed by rumbles that she can feel in her hands, as they travel from the ground through the car to the steering wheel; the hammering of the rain on the roof is deafening; the volume of water pouring down the windscreen renders the wipers useless. She turns her lights on in the grey gloom, they do little to help her see but she hopes that it makes her better seen – although the lights in front and out back are only smudges, bright but shifting in the droplets, rivulets, streams that envelop her car. With visibility so poor, the traffic slows to a crawl. This is when real accidents happen, she thinks, and grips the wheel tight. She's never driven in this much rain before.

She finally realises what the little traffic signs depicting an umbrella, white on blue, are for, as she drives past sodden motorcycle drivers huddling under overpasses and bridges. She remembers holding on to him at the back of a scooter in tropical rain on some island in the pacific, cleaving through a wall of rain. He couldn't have seen anything at all. They were on their way to or from the only launderette on the island and, whether clean or dirty, all their possessions must have been entirely drenched. Glad now she is in a car, surprised it doesn't leak, she is dry inside a little red submarine, making its way through a tempestuous sea. The rain comes in waves, each seems heavier, although such as thing as even heavier rain seemed impossible but a minute ago. Now it is almost as dark as night. She turns the radio off, to concentrate on driving, she could not hear it anyway over the din of the storm. She tries to follow the satnav as best she can, signs are barely legible, road markings all but invisible and she has to look out for traffic lights. The journey takes over two hours.

She arrives at the car rental office, at the edge of an industrial estate. The rain shows no sign of easing. Rumbles of thunder in the distance makes her worry about the girl back at the house, who is scared. Thunder is so very loud here, she wonders where the dog is hiding, she seems to favour their bathroom, as far under the sink as possible. She has a heard a theory that dogs hate thunder because they sense the electrical charge, and thus seek places that are earthed, near metal structures, pipes, water. It seems to make sense, the girl likes to hide in bathrooms during thunder, finding herself a Faraday cage. The safest place to be during a thunderstorm is a car, so maybe she should have brought the dog, would she have felt safer in a car?

She parks close to the entrance to the office and runs in. She should have brought an umbrella. The office is large and cool and quiet and almost empty, a man sits at the front desk and she can see a woman sitting further inside in front of a computer. She states her errand. The man at the front is the man who insisted on the phone that she come in, and he asks her to hold on a minute and disappears into the back of the office. She is relieved, he seems to know what needs to be done, she sits down, expecting to be given some forms to fill in while somebody has a look at the car. She feels sorry for the somebody having to go out in the pouring rain. Perhaps she'll have to wait until the rain stops, so they can have a good look. She sighs at the thought of the delay; she just wants to go home.

To her surprise the man emerges with a large umbrella on his arm.

'We need to go to other office,' he informs her.

'Why?'

'To fill in paperwork.'

It is unclear why this can't be done in the office they are in. Her questions are met with little more explanation than that which has already been given, so she gets up to follow.

'Where is the other office? Is it far?'

'You drive, I show you.'

She is surprised, but what can she do? They go to the car, sheltered by his umbrella, she gets in the driving seat, he next to her, and they set off. The man says nothing but gives her brief directions, turn right, turn left, straight on. They drive further into the industrial estate, office blocks thinning out, replaced by low units, workshops, factories, garages. It keeps raining and she is feeling a little uneasy. Should she have refused, insisted that the paperwork could have been done in the office she arrived at? Too late now, he directs her into the drive of a small, rather ramshackle building. A mechanic's garage, a few vehicles in front. The double doors are open and he directs her to drive inside. This unit looks nothing like another office, it is built out of breeze blocks with a tin roof, there are hardly any windows, and the rainy gloom from outside is deepened in the corners of the workshop full of tools, machines, parts. Grimy and dusty. In one corner there is a small separate room. He invites her to go in.

'My colleague will help you with the paperwork,' he says.

A small man sits behind a desk in the tiny room. He is wearing black rimmed glasses and looks at her from under the beam of a lamp on his desk. His chair is almost wedged between two filing cabinets, she wonders how he actually got in behind the desk. As she enters the room she immediately finds herself between two chairs. If she wants to let the man who directed her here come in, she has to sit down in one of them.

'Please sit.'

She does. The rain is still pelting down outside, making a loud rattle on the roof. She only notices the small window at the back of the room when lightning makes it flash. Thunder rumbles over them. As the bolt makes her look up, she realises there are tanks of fighting fish everywhere, some on the desk, more on the filing cabinets, and on shelves above those. She counts thirteen tanks. Not unlucky here, she thinks. The man that brought her sits in the other chair. He speaks to the man behind the desk in Hokkien Chinese. She listens to the rain and looks at the brightly coloured fish in the tanks and wonders when she accidentally entered the world of Blade Runner.

'My colleague will help you fill in the forms,' the man from the first office says, and rises to leave.

'What forms?' she asks. She is not sure why she should need help with standard forms.

'The necessary forms.' He leaves.

The man behind the desk shuffles a pile of papers in front of him. He pushes one over to her side.

'Fill in name, address here. Sign here and here.'

'What is this?' Suddenly she is afraid. Is this some scam, some ruse to make the gullible *ang moh* wife sign her life away? She has always been careful what she signs, ever since working for the reclaim department of a finance company in her youth, calling up customers that had defaulted on their payment, explaining that yes, even though the photocopier-coffee-machine-printer that they had leased is no longer working, they still have to pay, their finance agreement is separate from the service agreement, it states so clearly on the forms they signed, if they don't pay legal papers will arrive in the post. To this day it was the worst job she has ever had.

'You need to sign this,' the man insists.

She looks over the first form, it looks like standard stuff from the car hire firm. She enters her details and signs, returns the paper to the other side of the desk, glancing at the intricate fins of the small fish in the tank on the desk. The man passes another piece of paper to her. This looks more official, or rather like a bad photocopy of an official form, the crest of the police at the top, smudged by Xerox reproduction.

'You fill in details here.' He flips the paper over. 'Here you draw accident.'

'I do what?' She looks at the blank space left at the bottom of the page.

'You show how accident happen. Your car here. His car there... Here you sign. You must sign.'

'But why? I don't know what this is.' She tries to skim read the form, tries to understand what she is signing, but can't quite make sense of it. There seems to be a clause that authorises someone – space left blank – to make a claim on her behalf. This man? He does not seem to be working for the rental firm. Who is he anyway?

The man behind the desk sighs. He looks tired and sad. In heavy Singlish he informs her that the other driver refuses to take blame, so the matter has to go to the police before it can be settled with the insurance company. She needs to fill in forms for the leasing company, for the insurance company and for the police. The car needs to be taken to the police to be inspected. This is not what she expected. This has taken more than ten minutes.

'Usually you need to go to police. We make it easy for you. Help you sign the forms. I will take car to police later. But you must sign forms.'

The way he says it makes her suspicious. She gleans that technically she needs to make a deposition to the police in person, but here they are getting her to sign some kind of proxy. She is not sure it is a wise thing to do. She knows how strict Singaporean law can be, should she not try to do this by the book?

'I don't understand this, I don't want to sign,' she says, putting her pen down.

He sighs deeply again. 'Then you have to go to police office yourself. Within twenty-four hour.'

She balks at the idea. Finding the correct place, getting there, waiting in the inevitable queue, explaining her case, filling in the forms. Definitely more than ten minutes.

They seem to have reached an impasse. She looks at the fish.

'Your fish are very beautiful,' she says. 'They are fighting fish, right?'

'Yes.' He seems a little surprised at first. 'But I don't keep them for fighting,' he adds quickly.

She is not convinced he is telling the truth but decides to play along.

'Ah, for their beauty? They are incredible. You have a very beautiful collection. How many do you have?'

He tells her he has twenty-eight fish. She asks if he has kept them long. He tells her all his life and his father kept them too. She asks about the different colours. He tells her about the kinds of betta he has. It isn't a long conversation, but it makes them both smile.

'So these forms,' she says, 'I don't understand, I don't want to have problems. The man at the firm said just a quick form and look at the car, nothing about the police.'

He has softened to her. 'Ah yes. I don't work for the firm. I am just a mechanic. But I do some work for them sometime. When there is not enough staff. Help with customers.' He sighs.

'So you don't want to be here and neither do I.' she says. She has softened to him.

She asks again about the forms. Why does the young driver of the other vehicle deny responsibility? Surely the law is clear? He concurs, he does not understand why. The man will naturally be found the guilty party and his insurance premiums are bound to go up. It is stupid. They agree. But she still must go through the motions with the police report. If she doesn't sign the proxy form, she'll have to go, he can take her, but it will be several hours wait in the police station. She does not want to go to the police station, she just wants to go home. She sees a tired man behind his desk wanting to go home too. She skims through the forms again: they look kind of legit. She decides to fill in and sign the way he's told her.

When she has finished, he asks if she wants a drink, a cold tea? Yes, she does. He motions to go out of the office and takes her to a dirty old fridge at the back of the garage. It is full of cans of iced tea. She takes one. She notices there are other fish tanks in the garage. She looks and admires the fish. He asks if she wants to see the ponds outside, and she does, but it is still raining, so he just opens the back door, and she peers out to see several large ponds of fish at the back of the building. Koi carp, he says. They are very pretty, she says. He smiles. She thanks him for his help and the tea. She does not think he will defraud her; she is but a cog in a different scheme. They want to fix the minuscule scratch on the back of her car, he says. They must take the vehicle in. She almost wants to argue, can't they do it after her lease is finished, it is hardly noticeable, makes no difference to her. But she decides she has argued enough with this man, it is just easier to go along. She wonders how much they'll charge the other driver or his insurance company for the repairs.

'I have to get home though,' she says.

'Yes no problem, you drive home, they come with replacement vehicle tomorrow. Someone call you.'

It's a hassle but less of a hassle than expected, so ok, she says. She thanks him again and takes her iced tea can into the car with her. She sips it on the way home and it is unbearably sweet.

The next day they bring the replacement car. It is the same small model Honda that she already has, but it must be somebody's personal vehicle. It is jet black, and has a spoiler on the back, shiny alloys, extra dials on the dashboard and blue lights that come on underneath the car when you open the doors. It also has ridiculously strong air freshener stuck to one of the air vents that she has to remove, she can't stand the smell. She is more worried about doing damage to this car than she was to the other, it is clearly somebody's well-loved motor. She wonders what he (it must be a he, but maybe she's wrong) is driving right now while she is driving his car. A bigger car or a bike? A week later she gets the little red car back again. Immaculately resprayed rear. She never hears from the police or the rental firm about the accident again.

8. Wild Rice

Sometimes she wonders if she is fit for living. She does things she knows will end badly and yet she doesn't take the two extra minutes to sort it out. I'm too lazy, she thinks, I'm after every shortcut. And what are they shortcuts to? Because what is there to do but to live well, rather than to live fast. What are those two extra minutes, anyway, lost into fifteen cleaning the mess, mopping the spillage, sweeping the shards of the broken plates. Is it dyspraxia? But she always has the thought, 'this will go wrong,' just before it does. She has the option, she can choose to take the dishes down from the rack one by one, to place the pan in her other hand down first, to clear the table before putting the full glass onto it. But she doesn't. She just goes ahead, aware of the potential consequences and then it breaks, spills, pours. Maybe it isn't about being too lazy to do things properly, maybe she is after the drama.

It is one of those American plastic bottles, 32oz, one litre or thereabouts, she estimates. One that proclaims it's free from some dangerous chemical or other. She cuts pieces of ginger and squeezes an orange into the bottle and then fills it with hot boiling water, to make a comforting and hydrating drink. She is sure she needs to drink more fluids, and this way is easier than just having endless water. It feels healthy and works as a hot drink as well as cold. Maybe she is missing the hot drinks of a temperate climate. The American bottle has a large opening and a screw-on lid attached to it by a loop in the same plastic as the lid itself. The bottle is now hot, filled with boiling water. But she could carry it a short distance. Or use a tea towel to protect her hands. She is heading to the cupboard to get honey and add a teaspoonful. She also wants some fruit. That means going back to the fridge. So she gets the fruit out of the fridge first and then grabs the bottle by the lid, open, dangling at its side. She is carrying the bottle simply by the loop attaching it to the lid.

She does think. She thinks: I should close the lid because the loop

47

could slip and this could spill all over the place, and what a nightmare that would be. And it's hot. Does she think that she could burn herself? Is that what she is after, a nice little emergency? A small injury to allow herself to feel sorry for herself and run to bed and pull the duvet over her head and cry?

Of course, the bottle slips through the flimsy loop, empties most of its contents over her lower right leg and crashes to the floor. It is plastic so the bottle doesn't break, but there is healthy hot drink across the floor, and the beginning of a tingling pain in her leg. For half a minute she stands there, baffled: she knew this was going to happen, so why did she carry it like that? She realises her skin is burning and that she should cool it down as soon as possible. She tries to mop some of the liquid up with one of the towelling mats that reside on the floor in local fashion, but as the stinging increases she stops short and rushes to the shower. Rather useless in the tropics, the water is cool only for a short while, then, becoming tepid, only serves to increase the pain. She rushes back to the kitchen, has another abortive attempt at mopping some liquid up with the mat, uses it to dry her feet, then opens the freezer. She grabs a handful of ice cubes and applies them to her leg. Blisters are beginning to form.

After the first application of ice the pain returns with some intensity. Looking at those blisters, she thinks she might need a doctor. Excitement grips her; it would be a break in the monotony of life. She could go to A&E and she would not have to cook or do the dishes. Soon she realises that she probably doesn't need urgent medical care after all, but she still considers calling him to say she can't take the dogs out, on account of the pain. Could he do it? It would force him to come home early, he would rush back if she made it sound serious enough. It would break the monotony, the loneliness, the everyday boredom. Just a little emergency, a bit of excitement, a moment of spontaneity. Jesus, she realises she relishes having scalded her leg with hot water because it is exciting. I need to find something to do, she thinks. A job. Or, God forbid, what my mother always says I need, a hobby.

She does yoga every Monday and Wednesday morning, sometimes Friday morning too, what else could be more stereotypically expat housewife? She doesn't like the Friday teacher, who seems to be showing off not only his physical prowess but his yogic wisdom, having them chant some sutras or do yogic breathing for twenty minutes, explaining the benefits of heating the system or whatever. It is not that she is not interested in the spiritual side of yoga, but here in this gym, any pretence of 'real' yogic insight seems false. Like all the ladies, and occasional gentleman, she is there to make herself look better. Perhaps feel better, too, but really it is the lure of long lean muscles and toned bodies that has brought them all there. Nevertheless, she enjoys the meditative parts of the class more often than not. A bit of relaxation in her busy day, she cannot but snigger ironically inside. Sometimes it just makes her want to cry, because it brings home the lack of any real pressure in her day, from which she would really need to relax. Of course, she's stressed, stressed by the lack of stress. Stressed by the emptiness and the monotony and a million things you worry about when you have nothing to worry about.

It's the end of class and they are all lying down in shavasana, corpse pose. Flat on the back, legs and arms relaxed, apart, feet falling to the side, palms facing upwards and gently curled in on themselves. Images of death. Five or ten or sometimes twelve corpses on the floor. If only corpses were so relaxed, so peaceful and so symmetrical. She imagines most corpses are not, but in some sort of aspect of writhing, contortion, or spasm. Violent deaths certainly do not yield shavasanas, but punctured, wounded, mutilated bodies, crumpled and crushed. She imagines a body in the bushes, on its back, and limbs askew, like a distorted shavasana. A knee bent to the right, arms both angled upwards, as if still trying to swat away a giant sting in the neck, a knife, a wound, staring eyes. No relaxation for the stabbed in the neck. And another body in the neighbour's kitchen. Its knees drawn up and the head pulled backwards, arms outstretched in impotent defence. A body on the floor in her house, on its side, arms pointing straight down along the body, eyes closed but mouth open. She stops herself imagining dead bodies, it is making her own body want to imitate those poses, play out those fantasies, pretend to be those corpses. She empties her mind.

'Relax your whole body. Feel your body sinking into the ground, pulled by the force of gravity,' the teacher is telling the class. She follows instructions, imagining the force of gravity pulling her prone body down. She sees herself lying here on the surface of a planet, a body massive enough to hold her firm to its surface, despite hurtling through space. She feels the ground, the mass, the earth, the pull. And suddenly her mind rebels, why should she be subject to this force exerted by a large quantity of dirt. Why is she condemned to be a creature, a being, so severely restricted in such a vast universe? She is shackled to a lump of iron and stone, in an infinite space, limited not only in her physical movement but in her mental reach by this arbitrary, fatal accident of existence. She ought to be able to stretch and roam across the universe, across space and time, truly free.

She has always felt like that. Since childhood. When she believed that after death all would be revealed, she thought her true being would be set free in her knowledge of everything. Including the knowledge of why she'd been imprisoned in her bodily incarnation, and what the point of it all was. So, death was not something she feared, then. Now, she is not so sure. To all intents and purposes death seems to be the end of existence. It makes this gravitational prison even more haphazard and cruel. How will she ever find out about everything? When will she ever be what she is meant to be? She should be god. What if she is and this is all there is? What if god is stuck on this lump of dirt and dies too? She's not relaxed at all when she rolls up her yoga mat and nods goodbye, slips on her flipflops and exits into the heat.

She hates supermarkets. She can cope with supermarkets if she is feeling well, but any underlying malaise, physical or mental, seems to be intensified, brought to the surface by the glare of the fluorescent lights of a supermarket. The bigger the supermarket, the worse it is. The excessive walking needed to locate items together with the excessive choice of products, and the inevitability of at least one particular item she is after being sold out, is devastating to her digestive and nervous system. If she is with him, which is not that often, she almost always needs the loo. She gets stomach cramps and cold sweats and has to locate the conveniences immediately. When she is alone it is a deep hopelessness that grabs hold of her. There is no relief for that. The longer she must spend in the supermarket looking for something on her list the closer to tears she is. Reorganisations of the layout of familiar supermarkets, which are not infrequent, are disastrous. Why do they insist on changing it all around, just as she has worked out an optimal route through the maze of jars and packets and piles of pineapples? She writes lists in an order tailored to the specific layout of the supermarket she is heading to that day. Vegetables and fruit first, then meat and dairy, then usually bread, after that it gets trickier. The dry goods and household items have less predictable placements in the average supermarket. Pasta before jams or canned fish after confectionery? She knows the reason, of course, for the changes, the constant unpredictability of details within a larger familiar scheme. They want her to go the extra mile, to pass something she didn't know she needed, on the way to picking up the things she has to buy. To stumble upon some more spending. There is, she knows, psychology behind even the layout of each single shelf, although she is not sure quite what it is. Premium brands at eye-hand level, cheaper variations less immediately placed, probably. If it was only that simple when it came to it, she would not mind paying more for a fast getaway. See, grab, pay. But there is more confusion. The recipe she found this morning calls for wild rice. She cannot see any wild rice on the rice shelf. There is white rice, long grain and short grain. There is brown rice, easy cook and difficult-cook. There is jasmine, basmati, thali rice, each white and brown. There is Uncle Ben's and various flavoured rice pouches. There are three kinds of risotto rice and two kinds of paella rice. There is cous-cous and quinoa but that is a whole other matter. There is red cargo rice – is that wild rice? It looks like wild rice. She doesn't know what wild rice looks like. Red rice looks like what she imagines wild rice would look like. Dark and hard and wild. The wolf among the sheep. It comes in five kilo bags. She does not want five kilos of red rice. There are so many grains and pastas in her cupboard, all spoiling in the heat and humidity, she does not want to add another variety to the collection. There is white rice in smaller quantities, but red rice and even brown rice comes in big bags only. Why would anyone want five kilos of red rice? Isn't it a bit of a speciality item, even here in Asia? She scans the shelf again for alternatives. She has been standing staring at the rice shelf for some time, she does not know how long, but it feels too long. Too long to be spending looking for and choosing rice, standing in the supermarket under the harsh lights, muzak humming somewhere above, people passing her with baskets and trolleys of goods on their way to the check outs, on their way out. She wants to get out too, but she needs some wild rice for the salad she wants to make this evening, white rice will get too wet, she has white rice at home, but it is not the right rice. She feels a lump in her throat. She doesn't know what rice to buy, there is too much rice. She wants to go home, to do something useful, something else than looking at rice, but she can't stop until she finds the wild rice. With tears in her eyes she perseveres, reads labels, cooking instructions, suggested recipes, serving ideas. She is nearly hyperventilating when she decides that she'll take five kilos of red rice, at least it won't go soggy in the salad, who knows if she can cook it in the rice cooker, but it doesn't matter now, she needs to get out. She manages to swallow the lump, blink away the tears and calm her breathing before reaching the cashier at the till. She remembers what she has forgot to buy off her list in her haste to get out of the shop. She doesn't care anymore. She doesn't care that the cashier is packing her shopping in a preposterous number of plastic bags, with only one or two items in each, she can't be bothered to say 'Stop! Please stop, the milk can go with the vegetables, the fish with the meat, they are all over-packaged anyway, vacuumed to within an inch of their lives, no cross-contamination will occur, and if it does, I'll take responsibility for any detriment to health that may be the result.' She just stands there and watches the packing of packets in layer after layer of plastic, the chicken, in its plastic wrapping, going in an extra small plastic bag before being placed in the plastic carrier bag with the supermarket logo on, like someone trying to hide a dead body of from view. Everyone knows dead bodies spread disease, be sure to cook it well, no pink bits or you'll get *salmonella*. Besides, the evidence of the death of the animal is there, the fingerprints and DNA of the butcher and the farmer and hers too, guilty of buying this poor animal for her delectation when it lived in a box all its life. Is it worth the pain of the animal, the dish you'll cook? Will it taste good enough for a being to have suffered its whole short and miserable life? You never even looked into its eyes; you couldn't wring its neck if you tried. Coward, glutton among a tribe of coward gluttons, she looks up and over the rows and rows of food in colourful packaging, a soothing uplifting song playing above it all. She feels like throwing up. She hands her plastic card over to the cashier, her little plastic token that gives her access to all these plastic boxes and bags of things she doesn't need or want, except wild rice, which is not part of the plastic kingdom today. She places all her plastic bags in her trolley and heads to the lift that takes her to her car. She unloads the bags into the boot and takes the trolley to the trolley bay to retrieve her coin, but the trolley bay is not for the supermarket she has just been to but for another vast emporium of stuff (maybe they'd have wild rice?) and she cannot, just cannot. She leaves the trolley and the dollar there and returns to the car, starts it and begins the spiralling journey out of the multi-storey carpark. As she drives round and round, each floor the same but with different coloured concrete pillars she thinks life never gets better, it is just this, over and over and over again, the same drudgery. In a few days another supermarket, another car park, another shelf she'll spend her life staring at, another chiller cabinet of flesh and plastic.

The only solution is to kill oneself. She thinks perhaps it's not such a bad thing, just to end it. She'll kill the dogs and herself.

9. Bikini and Crack

She has started enjoying exercise. It has been a gradual process, from overweight to rather toned. Spent her twenties getting progressively fatter, with a twenty-something's optimism of being able to carry it off, or work it off, or lose it any time she liked. As a child she had been chubby, then at some point she realised her belly was a belly and she 'needed' to get rid of it. There was a hiatus in the body fear and loathing in her late teens; she understood she was thin, when a male classmate commented that there was not much to take off her. Not everyone was wearing 27 waist jeans, her legs and torso looked good in the mirror, with or without clothes. She had no idea how it happened, but she'd become rather attractive, in a conventional way. It seemed for a brief moment as if her corporeal form approached the imagined spirit within, the one her childhood fantasies were made of: the elf, queen, the sorceress. She realises now that she'd simply hit that sweet spot in one's teenage years where the body conforms to beauty ideals. She thought it would last forever; it barely lasted until she was twenty. A student lifestyle of late nights and slept-away days quickly defeated the teenage sylph. The ladette culture was in full swing then, and she had never realised how impossibly toxic it was. Be one of the lads, but only if your body stays a girl. You can have fun but you cannot get fat. Let's not even talk about the sexual politics. It is your own fault, after all, for drinking all that beer.

Her body was never her priority, never a thing she really identified with since childhood. Every child has fantasies, but they play them out, enact them through their bodies. She kept hers in her head. An overprotective father, an emotionally absent mother, don't run, you'll hurt yourself, read books, educate yourself. Despite occasionally reminiscing about his own sporting prowess, her father encouraged none in her. Mental pursuits were safer, and as he offered her the unlimited horizon of the imagination, she never felt a lack for running or jumping or turning cartwheels. Not until school and gym class and all the other kids being chosen to the teams before her (why did they do that, let kids choose the teams, it was nothing but a ritual of humiliation, an exercise in hierarchy, a rehearsal of how-its-going-to-be: winners and losers?). But it was too late by then.

Bar some fads, in her twenties she refused to go on a diet. She laughed at the idea of Weight Watchers. Fat Club was for fat people. She watched her fatter friends go and fail and go. Perhaps this should have been an opportunity to learn about her body and accept, but to this day she remains a fat-shamer. Her own 'weight-loss journey' has made her less rather than more accepting of all the shapes and sizes. It was the way she was seen by others that made her change. Somebody, a stranger, nodded at her stomach and asked her if she was having a baby. She was stunned for a moment, regained her composure, and replied,

'No, I'm just fat.'

Choosing to lose weight was one of the most satisfactory things she had done in her life, along with her PhD. Proving her mastery of the body, just as she had proved her mastery of the intellect. Neither undertaking was glamorous, both involved submission to an institution. She joined the dreaded Fat Club and played by the rules, weighed her food and counted the points, and every week she offered herself to the scales like another chapter of a thesis to be judged by a supervisor. It felt like emerging from a fat-suit, like becoming herself again. It felt like victory. Triumphant, she bought a new wardrobe. When they got their first greyhound, she was relieved she had lost the weight, would not be the fat lady walking the skinny dog.

Now, for the first time in her life, she starts to push herself physically, and she enjoys it. For the first time in her life, she sees muscle under her skin, and she enjoys it. Finally, her body is responding, it is pliant. It goes further, faster. It performs the rituals of athleticism – push-ups, dips, burpees – she has never been able to master before. She relives some of the glory of those thin teenage years, but with an added sense of power, this time it is not simply bestowed upon her by youth and hormones, it is her own creation. She wishes she could have felt this at home in her body throughout all its shapes, but the truth is that now she feels that she inhabits her mortal coil more than ever, now that she can make it do things, contract and expand, work and play.

She still wants to be lean, but now she also wants to be strong. The new breed of women in action films, finally, are not simply thin women who pretend to punch but women who look like they can give somebody a bloody nose for real. But she also looks at men's bodies, because they are the ones that make the most damage. There she finds the muscles she wants, the strength, the aggression. She allows the perfect self in her mind to expand, bulges replace slim lines, wire and steel replaces undimpled skin. It's not that she wants to look like a man. She wants to punch like a man. She wants to kill like a man.

When she teaches feminist theory, she always tells her students: a militant feminist will refuse to shave her legs and advocate that women stop shaving their legs, in order to resist the patriarchal body ideals imposed on them by society; a critical feminist will ask why women feel that they need to shave their legs. Whether or not the critical feminist shaves her legs is irrelevant. As irrelevant, she hopes, as her own insistent depilation is to her politics. The sojourn in a climate that requires exposed legs and armpits reveals the weakness of her own convictions. She knows, of course, that it is simply a social construct that women should be hairless. At best simply a contemporary beauty ideal, at worst an insipid infantilisation of the sex meant to be weaker. She admires women who don't shave their armpits, although she notes two things: one, their choice is often still couched in the language of sexiness, as in 'mysterious, French woman with unshaven armpits,' thus changing nothing; two, the sweatiness issue is real here in the tropics. Less hair seems less sweaty. This is a good enough reason not to challenge patriarchy for the moment.

She is not sure in what way ideology makes her have her butthole waxed. Nobody sees it, of course, not even her husband. Neither of them is keen on anal sex. She finds the idea exciting, and will sometimes fantasise about it, but when it comes to the actual execution, squeamishness about excrement and pain scuppers any attempts. Nevertheless, anal hair bothers her. She doesn't know why.

Depilating the bikini line is tricky with the violent machine she uses for her legs and armpits; she has tried a few times and it has been a disaster. She isn't going anywhere near her butthole with that thing. So she tends to go every couple of months to have a 'bikini and crack' wax. She is glad the treatment is on offer, spelled out like that, on the menu of the beauty salon. In Britain she was not that bothered about explaining what she wanted but for some reason she feels shy about it here in Asia. Are Asian women less willing to talk about private parts, or she is just more comfortable with discussing hers with somebody from the same ethnic background? A strange kind of racism. She mumbles the 'and crack' bit when confirming the details with the salon when she arrives. What will they think of her? The request is clearly not unusual. She thinks, they'll think I'm into anal sex, but then she thinks, they'll just presume I wear a string bikini on the beach. What do beauty technicians think about when face to face with some strange woman's bits? Do they compare anal openings or are they thinking about their dinner?

All these questions go through her head as she undresses and lies on the treatment table. Yet she doesn't really want to know. Professional distance is a must in these situations. Like with doctors, you don't want them to be your friends, just to be there in their capacity as experts. There was that one time she had started therapy, and after a week or two the therapist had phoned her up to cancel their appointment. 'I've had a miscarriage,' she had said, and at that moment she knew she could no longer continue. The therapist had suddenly become real as a person, vulnerable and suffering, no longer just a disinterested ear offering objective suggestions on how to deal with her own pain. There on the table, face down and her legs apart, with a woman applying wax to her crack, she feels the same comforting detachment. Why is she is face down? It isn't the easiest way to access the area concerned. If she was on her back, pulled her knees up, and parted them slightly, her crack would be much more exposed. She thinks this, but she doesn't even think of asking. There must be silence between them, except for strictly necessary communication, like 'turn over,' 'open your legs,' and 'how far down?' 'What are you doing this weekend?' the waxing technician suddenly asks. Lying there, quietly thinking, she'd been relaxed, but now she feels herself stiffen. This is not the protocol. She wants to shut her undignifiedly open legs and cover herself up, but there is waxing in progress. She doesn't say anything; just wants to let the woman finish, thank her, go.

'Something nice? Going out?' the technician does not take the hint of her silence. She mumbles something about going out and eating, while waiting for the strip of wax just applied to be ripped off. When it's done, she closes her legs, and her thighs come together with a little slap. The woman says something about 'not yet finished,' but she swings her right elbow around and up with as much force as she can. She is aiming at the girl's head, but she can't really see what she is doing. It is mainly down to luck that she manages to connect at all, catching the woman's cheek with her elbow. She can feel the impact in slow motion. Skin on skin, very briefly, then the jarring pain of bone hitting bone, a jolt up to her shoulder, but she is pretty sure the waxing technician is feeling it even more. The woman staggers backwards, gasping.

Putting her hands in front of her on the therapy table, she pushes her taut body up. She is happy she has been doing all that yoga. She has her back to the woman still, but can hear the waxing lady inhaling to scream. 'Shut the fuck up,' she whispers loudly. As the beauty technician starts to wail, she pulls her legs in beneath her, jumps into a squat and quickly stands up, like a surfer popping up. The room is small, and she hits her head on the low hanging lights. Swearing, she ducks down and turns towards the sobbing woman. She takes a step to the edge of the table with her left foot and kicks the waxing lady in the head with her right. The woman gasps and redoubles the intensity of her screams.

A few weeks back they'd seen a fellow punch another fellow in the face. It had been in the new cafe on level two of the mall where the waxing salon is located. It was shocking to see, she'd felt her chest constrict. She'd been surprised at her own visceral reaction. Her body felt as if it was being flooded with adrenaline, ready, buzzing. She felt queasy for quite a while. An ambulance arrived, and the police. People where whispering to each other in the corners. This will give them something to whisper about.

Somebody will come in any minute now; she can hear them outside the door. She jumps off the table toward the beauty technician, pushing her down with all her weight, feeling something crack in the woman's bones as she crumples awkwardly beneath her. She punches the girl, who is cowering away from her, repeatedly in the back of the head. Her knuckles are really hurting. Somebody is opening the door, but they must just look in and turn around gain, because nobody is stopping her as she stands up and starts kicking the woman in the back, in the side. The waxing lady tries to get up, but she uses both her arms to push the hair removal executive back down towards the floor. It's not too hard, she is bigger, and her adversary is in pain and too scared or shocked to fight back. She kicks her in the head again. The woman stops screaming. She can hear people shouting and running outside. She is standing there, in a tank top with no skirt or pants on. She leans down, clenching her fists, exposing her newly waxed crack to the door.

'That's it, miss. Finished. See you outside,' the waxing executive covers her with a towel and slips out of the door discreetly. The woman didn't say much during the time she was applying wax and ripping it off the edges of her pubic region and right down in her crack. She wonders what the girl was thinking, but she doesn't really want to know.

10. Graham

He sees a dead snake on the road as he is driving home. It is entirely
flattened, run over by tyre after tyre after tyre. It is no longer a snake
so much as the shell of a snake, no, not shell, he thinks, shell is the
wrong word. A shell is hard or brittle and crumbles when run over. A
shell breaks and scatters, but what remained of the snake was still
there, complete, a tube squeezed out and its innards carried away in
the tread of all those tyres. Left on the road was the tough skin. It
makes him think of a dying dachshund in a novel he read once, he
cannot remember by who. Le Carré? It had the sense of exotic
locations and intriguing spies, but deflated, satirised, the dog's tongue
protruding like 'toothpaste out of a tube.' Not the glamour of James
Bond, but the mediocrity of a middle-aged Brit abroad. Once the
toothpaste is out of the tube you cannot put it back again. Yet the
eviscerated snake on the hot road had retained its shape, it was still
visibly, even iconically, snake-like, its body in three curves, at one end
the bulge of the head, the other end tapering off. Flattened, it had
metamorphosed from a real snake into the internationally recognised
sign for a snake.

He turns up the drive halting the broad black nose of his car just
inches in front of the gate. An automatic routine, his right hand knows
exactly when to start turning the wheel to the left (just as his brain
subconsciously registers passing the one palm tree on the road without
any leaves) and his foot knows exactly the length of time to slowly
depress the brake pedal (3.4 seconds or a certain hundreds of
thousands of brain impulses that he isn't aware of). His left hand is
already fumbling for the gate remote control. The lights are on in the
house and outside, illuminating the blue pool. He can't see the pool
from the front drive, but he knows what it looks like. He never swims,
but likes to look at that luminous blue rectangle in the evening, ripples
on its surface casting shadows of light and dark at the bottom.

His wife is home and so is his daughter, back from school, studying in her room. She studies too much, he thinks, but he doesn't say anything. They, mother and daughter, spent two weeks back in the UK last month, driving from university campus to university campus, doing the open day rounds. No clear favourite has emerged. Uncertainty about projected grades a factor perhaps, not getting one's heart set on one place. The courses all vary slightly, too, and doesn't the opportunity of a year out in industry weigh heavier than the quality of the showers in the student accommodation? America is a possibility, although he is not sure he wants to encourage it. He is not sure he wants to encourage anything.

'I made lasagne,' his wife says as he walks into the kitchen. 'Joe is at practice, and Andrea is eating in her room.' She is wiping the stove top and washing up the pots and pans used for the preparation of the lasagne, which has apparently just come out of the oven. The lasagne is one of his preferred dishes among those that his wife cooks, or was when they lived in Berlin. Here he finds it heavy and hot, but he doesn't say, hasn't said any of the many times she's cooked it for him, and now he doesn't want to say. He turns the air conditioning down a degree.

'Lovely,' he says.

The lasagne is in a square ceramic dish, and she cuts it into four pieces. She plates up three of them and covers the rest in aluminium foil. She grabs a knife and fork from a drawer and disappears upstairs with one of the portions. He can hear her voice from Andrea's room, asking if she wants something to drink. The answer is negative. His wife reappears, takes more cutlery out of the drawer, and puts the remaining two plates on the dinner table. It looks big and empty with only two places set out.

He is shuffling the unopened envelopes of the day's post, one behind the other. He's sure he's lost track and looked through the pile at least twice, when he realises his wife is saying something.

'Sorry, darling?'

'A package came for you today. There,' she points to a long, thin cardboard box on the kitchen counter. He drops the letters and picks up the box, which has his name and address on it. It's not very heavy. He tries to open it, but its taped shut very thoroughly so he rummages through a kitchen drawer.

'What are you looking for?'

'Scissors?'

'There.' She points to a pair on the counter opposite.

He cuts the tape at the short end of the package but still can't get the cardboard open, so he cuts that too. He tries to shake whatever is in the box out through the end, but it is stuck, he can't even get it out with his fingers. He cuts along one side of the box and prises it open like an oyster. Inside, in a clear plastic bag is a matte grey aluminium rod with a black rubber handle on one end, and two concentric white plastic circles at the other. He looks at the object but can't work out what it is. He takes it out of the plastic bag, and realises that the aluminium rod extends, telescopically, and the two circles swivel in two directions making what looks like a small gyroscope. He takes the thing by its handle, holds the rod in front of his face and stares at the contraption. The gyroscope is about the size of a golf ball.

Suddenly he realises what it is.

'Ah, the picker upper!' he says, smiling.

He extends the rod and jabs at the floor.

'Wine?' says his wife.

'Yes. Yes, please.' He presses the sections of aluminium back into each other, lays the picker upper on the kitchen counter by the post and sits down at the table. She fetches a bottle from the wine fridge and pours him a glass, perfectly chilled to 18 degrees, a temperature the glass of wine will maintain for approximately two minutes. They eat.

They sit at the table between the kitchen and the living room, the rooms barely delineated by the hint of walls. Someone who lived here before knocked the walls down. Opened the house up, let some air in. Then shut the heat out with large glass doors and turned the aircon on.

She tells him about her day. About some woman whose dog got

63

injured and that Dr Birming, who operated on Billy, had performed the surgery. You get what you pay for, in the best hands possible. He looks at Billy, asleep flat on the cool tiles in a corner of the kitchen, next to his dog bed.

'But I don't think he's that fat,' his wife says.

'No, but he's still limping. Better make it easier for him...' he starts uncertainly, 'not *increase* his load...' His wife had been visibly upset when the vet had pronounced Billy overweight, but he agreed with the vet, Billy was fat, no wonder the poor bugger's knees were giving out.

'Well, you take him for a run tomorrow,' she starts clearing the plates away.

'Ah,' he says. A wave of guilt shoots through his stomach, heavy with the pasta and meat. Despite the aircon he feels beads of sweat on his forehead and neck.

'Something... So sorry.'

'Ah,' she also says, but with a different inflection, as she places the plates into the sink with perhaps a little less care than usual. But as she turns back to him her face is relaxed. Maybe he's imagined it. 'Fine, no problem. I can go with Andrea, she has a study day tomorrow, a bit of fresh air will do her good.' She picks up her empty wine glass, takes it to the sink and starts washing up.

'I have to go to New York tomorrow.'

'Oh.'

'Sorry such short notice again, Rob was going to go but then decided I better go, big deal, you know how it is.' He had known for several days he would have to go, Rob was never meant to go, but for some reason, he wonders why, like always, he has waited until the last minute to tell Helen. He hasn't told Helen it is pretty much a job interview, either. A good possibility for a promotion, a hike in salary and another move across continents. He'll be glad to get out of this infernal heat.

He goes to the sofa, taking his wine glass with him, and turns the TV on. Joe comes home, sweaty from football practice. He chucks the gym bag he is carrying on the floor in the kitchen and disappears off upstairs, announcing he's having a shower. Helen shouts, 'There is lasagne!' up the stairs after him and then goes back and picks up the bag, takes the damp clothes out and puts them in the washing machine. She scoops powders and pours liquids into the machine, turns a knob, and presses a button. It beeps and starts making whooshing sound, sucking water into its insides. She goes back to washing up. The water running in the washing machine and the water running in the sink and the hum of the aircon all create a wall of white noise. He has to turn the sound on the TV up to hear the commentary to the football game he has found on one of European satellite channels he got for his kids to never watch.

'Can you turn that down a bit,' his wife says. 'Why do you need someone to tell you what the players are doing? Can't you see?'

He can see, even though he doesn't really care who wins. He turns the sound down. It's too warm for red wine but he takes a sip out of his glass anyway.

Joe comes back down, his hair wet and uncombed. He is wearing a white T-shirt, dark blue shorts, and flip flops. Joe throws himself onto the sofa next to Graham and Graham quickly has to lift the arm attached to the hand holding the glass of wine, to avoid spilling it on himself. He checks the front of his shirt for any stray drops. There is a small stain of tomato sauce. Joe puts his feet up on the coffee table.

'Who's playing?'

Before he can answer his wife is there with a plate of lasagne for Joe, and asks if Joe wants a glass of water, which he does.

'I'm parched,' Joe says and starts telling him about a goal he scored at practice, and he's forgot his question about the teams, which is lucky because Graham is not sure he knows who is in fact playing. He squints at the 55-inch Ultra HD TV and tries to make out the two three-letter codes in the left-hand upper corner but can't. He needs glasses. Or maybe he's just tired. And hot. Does heat affect one's eyesight? Expands the liquid in the eyes, perhaps. Altitude does, the lesser pressure changing the shape of the eyeball, he knows, but heat, he's not sure.

Helen has finished washing up and joins them at the other end of the sofa, sitting down gently with a glass of water in her hand. She takes a magazine from the coffee table and starts turning the pages.

'The car needs new tyres,' she says.

'I got new tyres last month,' he says.

'No, not your car. My car,' she says.

'Ah,' he says.

Joe is eating his lasagne and watching the football and Helen flips the pages of her magazine and he takes a sip of his wine.

Andrea comes downstairs and places an empty plate and a fork in the sink. Helen gets up and goes to the sink to wash it up, and Andrea takes her place on the sofa.

'I hate biology,' she says. 'I don't even *need* biology. I'm doing economics, like, when am I *ever* going to need biology? Not in my job or anything.'

'Are you going to the Gardens by the Bay East with Billy tomorrow?' Graham asks nobody in particular. 'If you do, can you take the picker upper?'

A golf course runs the length of the land side of Gardens by the Bay East. A tall, netted fence divides the two, but it isn't quite tall enough. A number of stray golf balls land in the parkland. Graham picks up every one he can find. He looks forward to finding golf balls when he takes Billy for a walk, prefers to take him to the Gardens rather than the golf ball-less beach.

'Mhm, sure,' says Helen.

Andrea doesn't seem to have heard him.

'What is a picker-upper?' says Joe after a while.

'Aha!' says Graham and leaps off the sofa. He grabs the aluminium rod from the kitchen counter and extends it as he walks back to the sofa and around to stand in front of the TV. He jabs at the ground.

His family stare at him.

'You're in the way, dad,' says Joe.

'What?' says Helen with a scowl.

'Golf balls!' Graham jabs at the ground a few more times, looking at his wife.

'How many golf balls can you possibly need, Graham?' she says.

'And why can't you buy them like normal people?'

'How much did you pay for that?' his daughter suddenly asks, interested.

'I don't know, twenty five dollars?' he replies. 'With shipping.'

'How much is a golf ball?'

'Ooooh. Well, a decent one. Maybe forty dollars for twelve or so. They're pretty pricey here.'

'So just over three dollars each,' Andrea was always good at mental arithmetic. 'So you have to pick up eight of them to make it pay for itself.' Graham smiles and nods at her. She had a good head for business, his daughter, just like himself. He suddenly stops smiling, as if he has just thought of something important he has forgot to do.

'For chrissake dad, you're in the way!' Joe is leaning to the left and right, in exaggerated movements, holding his empty plate in front of him.

Graham goes back to the kitchen, folding the picker-upper in on itself again. He stands and stares at the pool outside of the patio windows, but he doesn't go out. The underwater lights and the tiles make the pool appear impossibly blue, like an imagined sky or a tropical sea on an old, hand-coloured postcard. Tiny waves on its surface make a pattern of darker patches and lighter lines, a wobbly net of nuances of blue and clear. Suddenly he wants to immerse himself in the water. He can't remember ever using the pool in the years they have lived here, but tonight he wants to. He has watched his children splash and laugh in the pool countless times, sitting beside it, sweating in the shade, but tonight he wants to wash the sticky film off his skin in that blue water. He could go up now, change into his swimming shorts, although he's not entirely sure where they are, he hasn't used them in so long, and come back down and jump in the pool. He could ask Andrea if she wanted to join him, maybe get that inflatable crocodile she had.

'I'm off to bed,' says his wife just behind him, making him jump.

He hadn't realised she was there. He turns around but she is already walking away from him.

'Yes, me too. It's late, got to get up early tomorrow, get to the airport before the traffic,' he replies. He looks at the pattern of light in the pool for a few more moments, before following his wife upstairs. In bed, he reads for a while before turning the light off, a few paragraphs from a novel somebody recommended. He is sure he read the same page last night. Just before he falls asleep, he thinks of the snake on the road.

.11. Baba Ghanoush

She is roasting aubergines and considering the problem of killing. It is a way of making cooking more fun. For Chinese New year she bought a large gas grill for the patio, one of those hulking americo-antipodean things that her husband turned his nose up at on account of it being too easy, requiring none of the time, effort and mess of the trusty old Weber kettle barbeque they had for years in London and used fewer times that they have fingers to count on. For that matter they have used it only two or three times here in the tropics. It is altogether too much of an event, done on special occasions, with preparation and lighting and burning and unpredictable cooking times. The point of the gas grill is for it to be an everyday cooking device. It has three burners, a half-and-half cast iron grill and hotplate (reversible), combo and a side burner. It is made of matt black metal and has a lid with a thermometer. And it makes her feel a bit tarnished – no, tarred. Tarred with the same brush as other expats. Just another housewife with her garden and her patio and her massive grill, and nothing better to do than to roast aubergines at ten in the morning. She is not like that. But of course she is. Buying a gas grill was not as easy as you'd think in a country with all-year-round barbeque weather. Ninety percent of Singaporeans live in flats or, if New Year wishes come true and they are prosperous enough, in condos, perhaps cluster houses. There are barbeque facilities in communal areas and public pits in many parks in the city, easy to book via an efficient electronic system. For most residents of the city barbequing is a convivial affair. She, on the other hand, is grilling alone.

She checks on the aubergines. They are getting quite charred on one side so she turns them over, exposing their purple skin to the flames. She remembers that you are meant to prick them so they don't burst, goes inside, stepping over the dog lying in the patio doorway, gets a skewer from the kitchen and comes back and stabs the aubergines. They sizzle gently. She keeps staring at them as they char black outside and leak juices from the soft oozing flesh inside. Like a burned decomposing body, she thinks, and what a clichéd morbid thought that is, at least the aubergines smell better. She takes them off the grill and cleans it with a wire brush. It is a much more pleasant space to cook, out here on the patio in the morning breeze, than in the hot wet kitchen. And more sociable in the cool of the evening when he is back, to be able to cook and talk and have a glass of wine. Recreating the rituals of middle-class life in a new climate. She is no better than Robinson Crusoe recreating a world of private property, production and capital on his deserted island. Is it a human need, to make a new world into an old and familiar one, she wonders? At what age does one become so settled in one's ways that one has no choice but to remake the old wherever one goes? At what age, she wonders, could you take the woman out of bourgeois London but not bourgeois London out of the woman? The academic housewife, the champagne socialist, critiquing her own ennui.

She immediately rebels at her own thoughts. What if she simply likes drinking wine and chatting to her husband while grilling prime cuts of meat. Those are nice things to do. What if the basic economic relationships of the world are essentially capitalist: to survive we need to consume, to consume we need to produce. Except hunting and gathering, of course. Like the dogs. No private property, no working the land, no production, no bosses no workers no class war. Only successful hunts or starvation, and life somewhere in between. She isn't convinced. And yet this is the life she has fetishized in her relationship to the dogs. The ease, the directness, the connectedness – and it would provide a solution to the ennui. No time to be a bored housewife when you have to hunt or gather. Or die.

The thrill of the hunt.

The charred aubergines have cooled. She halves them and scoops out their flesh, stringy and a colour somewhere between green and brown and dotted with small seeds, into a sieve above a bowl. She pulps the flesh with a fork, forcing the remaining fluid to drip down into the bowl. Is this not the opportunity she never knew she had waited for? A place where she is little known, a place divided and segregated where she is in a class less likely to be suspected, in a group treated, she expects, with some tolerance by the law. So she imagines, although she also wonders if there is not the risk of being made an example of. But that is not the point, because the law will not be involved. The point is, is she not in an ideal position to avoid suspicion, detection? If the killing is random enough, far enough from her own sphere of this life of outside grills and evening glasses of wine, who will suspect a housewife? She bristled at the description when they went to open a bank account, and upon hearing she had no current employment, the clerk had entered 'housewife' on the application form under her name. She does not want to be a housewife, but she will let them think that she is.

While the aubergine flesh drains she takes a lemon out of the fridge and squeezes the juice out of it. She takes a jar of tahini out of the cupboard, attempts to mix some of the risen oil back into the sesame seed paste, gives up and combines one teaspoon of it with the lemon juice. She crushes a clove of garlic and fries it quickly in olive oil, then mixes it with the tahini and lemon. She spoons the aubergine flesh into the mixture and stirs.

She starts carrying a knife on her morning walks to the Gardens by the Bay East. When she was a teenager, a friend bought her a flick knife in Germany. One of those standard locking blades, about 10 cm long, with a pearl handle. There was a pea-sized release button in the middle of the handle, and two small, curved commas of steel at the top of it like the cross-guard on a sword. The blade flicked out with satisfying power when you pressed the button. She used to carry it when she went out at night, it gave her a sense of security. She imagined a male attacker, a rapist jumping out of a bush or stalker following her in the night, and how she would deal with them with the knife. As she walked home from the underground station in the dead of the night, she used to flick it open over and over. She listened to music on her discman and timed the flicking of the knife to dramatic moments of the soundtrack. It put her in a starring role in the film in her head. No doubt she would have been clueless or paralysed with fear had she actually been attacked. It never happened.

The knife still feels nice in her hand, it has a reassuring weight. She has to oil its hinges a little, it was getting slow. The spring is probably not as taut as before, but after the oiling its action is swift enough. It also fits in her pocket. She does not play with the knife now, but holds it inside her palm in her pocket, feeling it grow warm in the morning heat. She only carries it in the mornings and only in the Gardens by the Bay East. This is when and where it has to happen. She doesn't go there every day, keeps going to the beach now and again as she has always done. She has time, is patient. There are many circumstances that need to be right. She starts going a little earlier, she knows that is when he is there.

That fellow with the overweight retriever; in her mind's eye he always wore red chinos. He seems a man that would wear red chinos and a jumper slung over his shoulders. Unlikely attire in the heat, but her imagination imposes that stereotype on him. They met walking the dogs, just him and her and their dogs, and chatted a while. He asked what her husband did but never what she did. It incensed her. His wife, who she met most days, was a nice lady with whom she has absolutely nothing in common except being an expat wife. A woman who spent her time getting two teenage kids to school, walking the dog, and who knows what else? *She* spends her time making baba ghanoush.

She considers where it would best be done. Although early in the morning the Gardens by the Bay East will be fairly empty of people, bar the waterfront walk, much is open ground. Initially she thinks of simply doing it at any point when there are no people around. Walking along with the dogs, chatting, keeping an eye out. Then turning around pulling the knife from her pocket, flicking it open and stabbing him in the stomach. She is hoping that the shock would preclude any resistance, that the injuries, even though unlikely to kill instantly, would prevent pursuit. She will simply turn around and walk away, softly calling the dogs if they don't immediately follow. She will continue on her walk, turn around as usual and then, walking back, come across his lifeless body and call the emergency services. She will dispose the knife in one of the ponds. If she calls the emergency services after she 'finds' him, she'll have an excuse for any blood on her clothes. Hopefully not too much blood in case anyone one sees her before the find. She decides to wear black.

The scenario is problematic, however. She will have to wait long enough for him to die. If he is in an open area somebody may notice him and call for help and save him before she got back. After some thought she decides to stab him in one of the thickets of palms and reeds that fringe the ponds, more sheltered spots. No doubt if she pretends to see something in there as they are walking, and feigns real interest, he will be curious enough to investigate. Cursory research reveals that stabbing to the back has less fatal outcomes. If he goes into the bushes before her, she will have to make him turn around before being able to stab him in the chest or the stomach. She realizes then she does not even know his name.

The next time she goes to the Gardens by the Bay East, red chino man is the one walking the retriever. She is prepared, but she is not ready. She only has the one dog with her, the girl is recovering from a deep flexor tendon tear. She feels a little incomplete without them both.

They walk along as usual, until the pond at the end of the park.

'What is that?'

'What?'

'That there, in the bushes. Is that...?' she walks, bending over with curiosity, towards the palms.

'There! Is that a...?' she pushes aside the heavy, dark green leaves, coarse and prickly to the touch, and takes a tentative step in.

'Oh my god!' She adds alarm to her voice, acting distressed, hoping to engage his male superiority complex. It does. She has his attention; he quickly moves forward past her.

'Wait, wait. Be careful!' she adds to the act with desired effect, the bastard is too much of a self-centred chauvinist to pay her any attention now. He has taken over from the woman, it is his investigation now, he needs to find out what it going on and sort it out. He dismisses her by stretching his left arm behind him, while he parts more palm fronds with his right arm. His fat retriever is curiously sniffing about at his feet. She considers her options for a second. Stab him in the kidneys now? Not deadly enough. Stab him in the side of the chest, on the left side, hoping to hit the heart? Not accurate enough and besides, her left hand would be too weak, her aim bad. The neck, it has to be the neck. A slit across the front of the neck, like in the films. But it requires some precision, and some force too, the cut cannot be superficial, it must sever the trachea and ideally an artery too. She is not sure she can do it; he is taller than her, he will shrug her off before she is finished. The only real option is a stab in the neck. She has felt the spot on her own neck many times, just under the jawbone, slightly forward from the angle of the jaw, where you can feel the pulse, full and warm, just under the skin. There, just behind the airpipe, if she's lucky she can cut that too, but first and foremost the carotid artery.

As she is thinking all this, she takes the knife, warm and heavy, out of her pocket. She glances at it very quickly as she presses the hard little button, and she cannot stop herself thinking about how she hates the clitoris being referred to as pea sized. She tries to change her grip on the knife with one hand only. Of course, she drops the damn thing. He is almost turning around as she stoops to pick it up, so she says, 'What *is* it?' which spurs his exploring ego on again. She adjusts the knife in her hand so that it is pointing diagonally up to the left out of her right hand, the back of which is facing her. She puts her left hand on his shoulder and quickly before he can react, jams the knife into the side of his neck.

He makes a sucking sound of surprise as he staggers backwards. She attempts to control the knife, to push it in further, to twist it, but it slips from her grip. He appears to be trying to clutch at it, but his arm and hand don't seem to be responding properly because he just manages to slap his own neck, like he is swatting at a mosquito. She starts to step aside, but as he falls his right elbow hits her in the chest, the right side of his body catching the left side of hers and pushing her to the ground. He is making strange 'kaaa... khaaa' noises now, and she twists herself free and kneels beside him. She wants to grab the knife again and make sure she finishes the job, but she sees his wide open pale blue eyes staring at her and she leans backwards onto her hands and watches him. The surprise in those eyes is quickly replaced by fear and then by emptiness. He is still making choking noises, but his hands go limp, so she presumes he has lost consciousness. She realises how much blood there is around her. On her.

She feels satisfaction. She feels panic. She stretches her hand out to pull the knife but hesitates. If he is still alive maybe blood will spurt out staining her further. She vacillates between waiting for him to die, which can't be long now, and taking the knife and getting the hell out of there. She decides on the latter, and pulls the knife out swiftly, as if she is ripping off a sticking plaster, and as she does, jumps back. She nearly stumbles into the pond. There is no big squirt of blood, like in a ninja film, just a copious leak. She wants to touch the blood with her fingertips and put her fingers in her mouth and taste it, but stops herself. She turns around and now she feels like she does when there is a ton of washing up to be done and she wishes she had a maid, and she could just sit back and have the maid do it. She just wants someone to deal with the mess. But she remembers this was exactly the kind of thinking that made her kill this man. The feelings of entitlement, the arrogance.

Except he didn't have a maid. That doesn't matter, he was that kind of man. She is not that kind of woman: she needs to embrace the mess and deal with it herself. The mess she made.

She starts by plunging the knife into the water and giving it and her hands and arms a wash. The water is a dirty brown with a green tint and smells that colour too. Never mind, she can always say she went in after her dog. She suddenly remembers the dogs. Hers is lying down only a yard or two from the bushes. It is not far from where they have their usual rest every time they walk this way. He's having a rest. He looks at her with a worried face, but his face is always worried. The retriever is sniffing around his master, licking him, whimpering. She ignores him. He's not her problem. She continues to wash, splashing water on her shins, which have blood on them too. Her arms and legs are turning brown with a green tint, with flecks of algae stuck to her skin. She keeps on washing. The dog would never go into the water, of course, but nobody knows that. He did once, chasing a lizard. He came back drenched, so he must have gone at some speed. The girl once tried to cross one of the ponds on lily-leaves. She must have thought they were a part of the lawn. She had a surprise drenching too. Since then, they are more careful. They have learned the topography of their new habitat. She needs to pull the dog into the water if the story of her own soggy state is to hold. She calls him over, and he knows from her voice she's about to make him do something he doesn't like. He knows things like that. She has to take a few steps out of the leafy area and grab him by the collar. She is getting nervous now, so she is brusque. He whimpers a little at the rough treatment. She drags him to the pond and pulls him in. She is in the water to her knees, he to his belly. It will have to do. She can't well be entirely wet. Lucky she is wearing black. The wet of any blood looks just like wet. She lets the dog go and he bounds up to shore with a sorry expression and shakes himself off. He stands at a distance while she finishes her ablutions. Now she mainly looks like she has been in a dirty pond. It will also have to do. Her dog's staring and the stupid retriever's whimpering will give her away. The retriever is running up to her and sitting at her feet, as he usually does, and then darting back to his owner, over and over. She must go.

She walks away, calling her dog. He follows immediately. The retriever follows too. She tries to shoo him off, first with her voice, then by stamping her foot at him. Finally, she gives him a little kick. Not very hard. She couldn't kick a dog. He keeps looping back to his owner, then to her. Her dog barks and lunges at him, but he does that all the time. The retriever knows he will do no harm and ignores him. She starts walking quite quickly towards the car. She suddenly realises the car, oh god, will get stained. When they had finally bought a car, they had bought the one car in Singapore with fabric trim, they usually come with leather here. Why she wonders, when it is stickier in the heat? Maybe because it cleans better. Perhaps once you pay the extortionate cost of the certificate of entitlement that is necessary to own a car here, you may as well pay a few hundred, or is it thousand, dollars extra for a nice trim. She doesn't even know how much leather seats cost. She doesn't even know how much a pint of milk costs. The other day in the supermarket she put some courgettes in the trolley. He was with her and noted the packet.

'Over $10 for a couple of courgettes?'

'I don't know,' she said, 'where are they from? There are some more here...' She realised the other courgettes were less than half that price.

'Why do they put the same type of vegetable in three different places,' she was still not concerned about the price, primarily.

'These are even cheaper,' he had found another lot.

'Get those ones then.'

'How many do you want?'

'I dunno, three or four, that's why I got the other ones, I don't want too many, they just go to waste,' she had shopped purely on quantity.

'Wait, these are actually similar price, per gram.' He had swiftly done the maths. He settled on the second lot, the cheaper version in the right quantity. She had simply grabbed the first packet she saw – maybe she would have noticed the price at the checkout, but likely not. She has no idea. She doesn't have to. She makes no money. She just spends it. Housewife.

The retriever is still with them when she presses the unlock button on the car remote. She opens the boot and takes out one of the brown battered cushions that are in there for the dogs. She uses it to dry her arms and legs, and to sponge any wetness, water or blood, off her clothes. The cushions are a good colour, the stains are only a slightly darker brown than the material itself. She replaces the cushions and tells the dog, who is sniffing the stone he always sniffs just before the end of the walk, to get into the car. He hesitates a minute, then jumps in, while she uses a foot to keep the retriever at bay. She doesn't look at the retriever, she just closes the car boot, opens the driver side door, gets into the seat, closes the door, turns the ignition. A fuzzy World Service starts up on the radio. It's time for news. She reverses out of the parking space. Beware of rear parked vehicle. She drives off home.

12. China Club

At some point he had donated some money to his alma mater, now he's forever branded with the symbol of the cash-cow in their files, and they get invited to lunch with the Vice-Chancellor, who is in town with his retinue for a milk-round, squeezing the teat that yields clever young people and later, when they're less young and perhaps less clever, their money. The lunch is at a private club, a restaurant that happens to be at the top floor of the skyscraper he works in. He is not a member. Before they left, parents of friends had asked what club membership his job came with. The answer was none, those days were gone. They even have to pay the rent themselves, and the maid too, if they'd want one.

She has to dress up, which she doesn't very often. It is one of the things she likes about being an academic, there is no need, nobody does. It is your brain that counts, not the clothes you wear. She tries hard to look the part for lunch but knows she will fail. She never gets it quite right. They get a taxi there but she manages to get sweaty just moving between the cool of the house and the car, and then the car and the lobby.

Fifty-two floors up. The elevator doors open, and they get taken from the demure vestibule to the blinding light of the private function room, sunlight streaming through the floor-to-ceiling glass window beyond which the city stretches. Every other woman in the room seems to have some kind if innate elegance, at ease in their crisp clothes, manicured nails, and grease free hair. How is it possible in this heat? They don't seem to be going native with the aircon at all. She gets offered a glass of champagne. At least she can talk, she knows she can do that. She does. There are some fellow academics there, some of the alumni, some from the delegation, they all wear name tags and hers says Dr, so she gets asked. She's relieved most of the crowd does not expect medical, but she still has to crack the joke about reading poetry to the imagined heart attack patient on a plane. 'Is there a doctor onboard?' Ha-ha. Does she work? No, it has been harder than expected. The Singaporeans prefer their sciences hard. The other doctors onboard, physics, economics, geography perhaps, even a surgeon, the ones with jobs, all nod and smile kindly. Could she teach English in a school? She could. But that's not what seven years of studying was for, she thinks. She prefers literature. Books. Adults. But they don't have much time for reading in this town. They work too hard.

She ends up talking to the wives. The trailing spouses. How is she finding it? She's getting used to the heat, air conditioning helps, huh? She is a bit bored, she admits. Singapore has made great progress in turning itself into a place of culture the last ten years, yes, true. And she is trying to find some literary people, her tribe, slowly she hopes to ferret them out, the Singaporeans that read and write.

She looks over the cityscape beneath. The midday sun is rendering it sharp and clear, every box of concrete and steel, every tarmac artery, every cluster of green. Further out, boxes of blue, orange, green, grey, endlessly repeated and stacked. The leaden sea beyond and on the horizon a string of tankers, like some grotesque jewels holding their black gold. She'd always felt apart, yes, if she was being honest, *above*, but never quite so distantly as here. She doesn't say this last thought out loud. She looks at the woman next to her. Later middle age, cocktail dress, blond hair, big rings with big diamonds. Bigger than hers. The woman is also looking out over the city, has she been listening at all?

'Do you have children?' the woman turns to her and asks. No, just dogs. The move was so much easier, she adds, in the silence after her reply. Although they were a faff, too, the cages had to be specially made, and—

'Why don't you have children, then?' The woman's tone implies that this is her answer to the earlier confession of boredom. 'Singapore is a wonderful pace to have children. So safe, so green. The travel. And the help is so cheap.'

It is not the first or the last time she hears this suggestion. Some spell it out more than others: it'll be something to keep you occupied, you may as well, when you can get all the help you need while they are small, then the school will be paid for, by the time you decide to return home you have ready-made, easy-care children, with an international education and a raft of healthy outdoors hobbies.

'Perhaps,' she says and smiles. It is time to sit down to lunch.

They sit at a large round table in a corner made of glass. The Vice-Chancellor sits at the join of the two windowpanes, as if it indicated the head of the table. The food is a kind of Chinese banquet of many dishes, but confusingly brought out pretty much each in turn, not all at once. There is no lazy Susan in the middle of the table. In front of each guest is a fusion of cutlery. Knife, fork, western spoon, Chinese spoon and chopsticks. She watches the guests navigate their implements with each course that comes. The Europeans use chopsticks for pretty much everything, even the rice, with varying degrees of success. The Singaporeans mainly use the fork and spoon, the ubiquitous cutlery of the food court and hawker stall, and occasionally chopsticks for dishes that come in appropriate bite size pieces. It is a strange inversion of ethnic customs. The whites persevere in picking the rice into their mouths grain by grain, in a mismatched effort at upholding cultural appropriateness and European table manners. The Singaporeans eat with practicality, why stick with sticks when a spoon is so much easier? The only Indian man at the table eats with knife and fork.

A typical Singaporean scene. White, yellow, brown faces all gathered together, celebrating success in education and career, and the resulting largesse. There is no Malay person there. She's still trying to work it out. The fact that Malay is the so called 'national' language baffles her, when obviously English is the lingua franca of the nation, and various shades of Chinese the most culturally dominant tongues.

Singapore is a multicultural nation, but it is clear that not all cultures are treated equal all the time. Work ethics seems to be the scale by which groups are judged. She is a little surprised at first when some ethnic Chinese refer to the Malays as 'less committed to business.' But the white expat population do nothing to disguise their idea that Singaporeans, by which they mean Chinese Singaporeans, are out to skive off work whenever they can. The Anglo-Saxons in particular wear the twenty-four-seven work ethic as a badge. Singaporeans do not deserve the badge, because they take long lunches, leave at close of business and always take the opportunity to get an 'em-cee'. Medical Certificate, liberally signed by private doctors for a small fee, for every little ailment. She can't quite place the Indians. The directly imported middle-class Indians, with an education good enough to join the white-collar brigade are hard-working enough for the Anglos, they work harder than the Singaporean Chinese. The Singaporean Indians are another story, and then there are the Malays. There are explanations of course, logical reasons for the pyramid of privilege. The Indians and the Malay are more family orientated, they had been told in a strange session of cultural training provided by the company on their arrival. The Indians and the Malay like spending time with their families and thus prioritise work less. It is all about priorities, after all. A Chinese father, so the story goes, does his duty by his children by making the most money he can (ah those avaricious Chinese), but an Indian, and in particular a Malay, has a duty to be there physically for his children, a laudable aim, but it means he will be late for work. Nothing to be done.

The Anglo father is a devoted one, of course, that goes without saying. She imagines that the Anglo father has moved to Singapore for the promotion, encouraged by the fact that work-life balance is rumoured to be better than in his city of origin. Now he is made head of his division here in Asia, he has the freedom to spend more time out of the office with his family. He is still available to his team of employees on the phone, of course. Working from home. The Anglo father prioritises his family, too, but still keeps an eye and ear on work. Hard-working families.

She cannot quite fit those other expats, who are never called expats, into the privilege spectrum. Those whose families are not even in the same country to prioritise. Different rules apply to them. Your maid works harder than you, but she is and will always be less privileged.

Intersectionality is suddenly real and confusing here in a way she's never seen before: race and gender and class entangle in ways she finds fascinating but difficult to clarify. South Indian construction workers, Philippino maids. Expat bosses with their stay-at-home expat wives. At either end of the spectrum the women exist at home. Domestic goddesses and domestic servants.

The blonde who suggested she have children is next to her at the table. She was hoping lunch would cut their conversation short, but the woman is telling her something about her maid.

'My helper is wonderful. When she first came to live with us the children were small, and very fussy, of course. They'd simply refuse the stuff she tried to cook. I showed her all the dishes I used to make at home. I don't use recipes, I just throw a bit of this and that in, but she wrote it all down, and I made it into a little book for her.' How does one write that down in a book, she wonders, how does one instruct a maid to cook spontaneously? 'That made my life so much easier. The kids were happy as long as she cooked something out of the book. It was like having my own Bolognese, or whatever, just there, ready-made.'

She finds this story uncomfortable, almost offensive. The female foreign domestic worker is the most invisible of people living in Singapore, confined to the home by her work. Not her own home, somebody else's home. And on top of this, her very identity as a domestic worker, a cook, is deleted, replaced? The word helper is symptomatic. It is meant to be more respectful, better than the old-world classist term 'maid.' Maids belong to the upstairs-downstairs divide, helpers to the global economy. Helper implies agency and choice. Help is given freely. An impossible inversion: the employer is the one in need. The expat wife, dependant in name and nature on her husband's employment, is also restricted to the domestic sphere. She sneers into her won-tons. Solidarity between women on the stairs? A smile as you hand the crying baby over, a tacit understanding of confinement in cages, whether guilt or rusty. Hardly.

'I had to be out all afternoon, but Mary was home, of course, so I saw no problem with them coming. But then they wanted cash on delivery, so I had to hand her the money. And I realised,' the woman's voice lowers to a whisper, as she leans closer. 'I realised, the cash for that case of wine was more than I pay her a month! It was terribly embarrassing. I get Richard to pick up the bottles from the shop now.'

She is relieved when the dinner is over, when they get home and she can take her smart clothes off and sit in bed in just her t-shirt and pants. She throws her skirt and blouse on the floor, not even in the laundry basket. She knows she should hang them up so they don't get creased, but she can't be bothered.

13. Mary

The bed stands against one of the long walls of the room, a shelving unit against the short wall next to it and obscuring part of the window in the opposite long wall. The unit works as a bookshelf, wardrobe, storage cupboard, dressing table, and bedside table all in one. There are clothes folded on the top shelves, and a dress and a shirt on one hanger, secured to the top edge, trail against the left part of the top four or five shelves. Middle shelves hold rows of books behind some containers of toiletries and beauty products. The lower shelves are full of boxes, in front of which is a jar of sweets. A small section of one of the middle shelves, next to the bed, is empty save for a few photographs and a bible. And a small plastic egg that rattles when you shake it. It is the yellow plastic container from the inside of a Kinder egg, the chocolate eaten and the toy inside assembled and lost long ago. The egg, on its side, moves almost imperceptibly in the air current from the fan mounted near the ceiling in the corner diagonally opposite the head of the bed. The contents of the egg are not very heavy.

In the other corner, directly above the suitcases wedged between the foot of the bed and the wall, a TV is mounted. It is on, showing what looks like the news, but the sound is turned down. Next to the suitcases, under the fan, stands a console table and a chair. At the back corner of the table, behind a pile of papers, magazines and books, is a statue of the Virgin Mary and a candle. The candle has never been lit. On the top of the pile is a booklet bound by a black plastic comb. The first page is covered by see-through plastic and spells out in twenty-four-point comic sans, 'FAMILY RECIPES.' Some of the A4 sheets of paper bound within the booklet are poking out, a little dog-eared. The wooden chair is pushed under the table as far as it will go with the large batik-printed sheet folded on its seat. The door next to the window is half open, as open as it ever gets, because the console table is in the way. The loud chirp of a lizard hidden somewhere in the evening darkness outside comes through the door and the window. The window is made of matt angled glass slats that can be opened or closed with a wire running one side of the window. They are always open. There are no curtains.

Mary's hair is wet, and she is holding a towel and a bottle of shampoo which she places on the shelf next to her bed. She is wearing a white t-shirt, dark blue shorts, and plastic flip-flops. She sits down on the edge of the bed and rubs her hair with the towel, kicking the door shut. She pulls out one of the boxes from the lowest shelf and takes out a Samsung Galaxy Note 4 and clicks the screen into life. There is a text: 'Call at 8?' She has to move a jar of face cream and the shampoo bottle she has just set down on the shelf to find her watch.

It is 7.30. She fastens the bright green plastic Swatch watch on her left wrist. It matches the colour of her flip-flops. She hangs the towel on a hook on the back of the closed door and picks up the booklet from the pile on the table. She rummages through the papers in the pile for a while and pulls out an opened envelope. She sticks her hand down the back of the pile and feels around but comes up empty. With a sigh she turns to the shelf and scans its contents. She moves the hanging dress aside and finds a few pens and pencils stuck in a small airline Coca-Cola can with the top removed. Taking out a pen, she sits on the bed, adjusting the pillow behind her back, then leafs through the booklet, adjusting some of the pages that are falling out. She studies the pages for a few minutes and writes a list on the envelope.

Minced beef, tinned tomatoes and lettuce for the spaghetti Bolognese and salad, there is pasta in the cupboard and fresh tomatoes in the fridge. Chicken breasts, carrots and broccoli. There is plenty of rice. Potatoes and fish, flour, for the fish and chips, she knows there are peas in the freezer. Oil for the deep fryer is running low so she adds it to the list. Steak and pepper sauce for the adults while the kids have the fish. Everyone has chips. Maybe she will make that cheesecake, so she writes down: digestives, cream cheese, cream. She reviews the list, adds milk and fruit and cereal for breakfasts, and sighs when she realises most of it will have to be bought in the supermarket. She prefers the wet market, where she can see and smell the meat and fish and vegetables, where she doesn't have to go up and down miles of aisles to find packets and boxes. She considers leaving the cheesecake out, but the kids like it, and the oil has to be the expensive stuff from the supermarket, so she'll have to go anyway. It is Thursday tomorrow so the list will take her through to Saturday and then she won't have to go again until Monday morning.

She glances at her watch, ten to eight, and the list is done already. When she had to think of things to cook it used to take much longer. People say they want variety but then they don't like new things. They say cook whatever you like, what you eat at home, but then they don't like pork. It takes some time to figure out what they like if they won't tell you, time and thought and inspiration she does not have at the end of the day. This is easier. No awkward silences after dinner. Although she never had any issues cooking for the kids, she always cooked what she had cooked for Ivy, and they always liked it. All of them. When she goes home now she is surprised when Ivy says no to the dishes. 'No, mum, I am not five anymore.' The kids here never stopped being five or thereabouts, never stopped loving her champorado in the mornings. In this house she sometimes makes it for herself, for breakfast on her day off. She leaves some in the fridge when she heads out, and she knows it will be gone when she comes back, the kids having had it as a Sunday treat.

It's only five to eight but she puts her finger on the blue Skype square on her phone anyway. She doesn't have to look through contacts, Ivy is at the top of the recent calls list. Ivy is most of the entries in the list. There aren't many other people she calls 'long-distance.' Perhaps if long-distance had been this easy twenty years ago, she would have a more varied list of calls made and received, but when she first left it was Ivy she spent her change on in the payphone. Bernardo would pick up, tell her all that Ivy had been up to that week. The new words, the bruised knees, the good grades. Now Ivy is at the other end, tells her about Bernardo, even though there is not much to tell. But these days you don't need words, she sees him wave to her from the chair in the corner of the room, wistfully smiling. She doesn't mind him not talking – is relieved, she doesn't have much to say to him these days either. What is there to say? She guesses, even hopes, he has remained silent for her sake, for Ivy's sake, the way she remained silent about everything else. She doesn't want to know; he doesn't need to know. It doesn't matter, only Ivy matters. That is what their marriage is all about. Taking care of Ivy. Giving Ivy a future.

The phone plays its little pretend dialling tune, its mock ringing. She can see her own face in the screen. She tries a few smiles, frowns at the lines they make at the side of her mouth.

'Hi nanay.' She is still frowning when Ivy's face appears large on the screen and her own withdraws to the corner.

'What's wrong, mum?'

'Nothing, darling.' She turns back to one of her many smiles. 'Just exercising my face. Have to keep looking young.'

Ivy laughs, puts her hands on the side of her face and pulls up, a grotesque face-lift.

'Plastic surgery at its best!' They both say the advert catchphrase at the same time and burst into laughter.

'How are you, mum? Did you see Aunty May? Did you go to the beach? Did you make the barbecue pork?' The way Ivy doesn't pause for breath between her questions makes Mary sure she isn't after the answers.

'Yes, yes, good. It was good. How are you? How is dad?' She briefly worries something has happened to Bernardo. Worries out of old habit, not that it matters anymore, not to her, not to Ivy, who looks after herself now, and looks after Bernardo. But there he is, in the corner of the room with his sad smile, waving as Ivy angles the phone camera towards him.

'Dad's fine, it's fine, I'm fine.' That breathlessness again. She has something to say. Mary may have only hugged and kissed her daughter once a year for the past twenty years, but she has spoken to her on the phone enough times to know every modulation of her voice, every hesitation, and every nervous stream of words, and the emotions behind them all.

'Ivy?' She draws the name out, angles her head and raises her eyebrows at the phone, at her daughter's face on the screen. She catches herself thinking, she has broken something at home, got into trouble at school, beaten up the neighbour's boy again. She glances at the photo of a five-year-old girl next to her bed. The same girl as on the screen, unmistakably, but Ivy on the Galaxy isn't a bashful child but a young woman smiling nervously.

'Sorry. What is it, has something happened?' Mary makes herself speak to an adult.

There is a pause.

'I've got a job,' Ivy finally says, smiling, but her smile is a little unsure.

It's not what Mary expected.

'That's wonderful!' She feels a wave of warm excitement. 'So soon. What hospital? Did you get the one in the children's hospital that you wanted? But the General is also very good.' It is her turn to speak without pause, she knows where Ivy gets it from.

'I did. Yes, both. But.' Ivy starts several sentences and finishes none.

'Both! You can choose!' Mary can't quite stop her excitement. 'Which one is best? General is closer but the children's hospital, that's what you've always wanted. I know the pay is not as good initially, but think if you specialise in a few years, then.'

'Mum.'

'But maybe you don't want to tie yourself down too early, better leave your options open, and save some of that money.'

'Mum.'

'And if you—'

'Mum!' Ivy almost shouts. Mary stops.

'I've got another job.'

'A third one!? You didn't tell me. You applied to, but you didn't want that one, so now you have general and—'

'No, abroad.'

'Abroad?' Mary can't quite understand. Ivy had applied for three or four nurse's posts in or near Quezon City. 'You applied to a hospital abroad?'

89

A pause.

'Not exactly a hospital. But it counts as nursing experience, I will be... nursing.'

Slowly a realisation starts to creep into Mary's consciousness. Really slowly, because she does not want to let the thought into her head, even though it is the obvious one.

'In fact, I will be using some quite specialist skills. The child, it's disabled. Not much, but a little. They wanted somebody with skills and who wants to work with children. A paediatric nurse, really, but they liked me, and I really like children, so. It's a great way to get experience *and* save some money,' Ivy has got going again, continues, looking at her mother's now silent face, something distant in Mary's eyes.

'I'll be able to save a lot of money, mum.'

'Here?' asks Mary.

Ivy looks away at something in the corner of the room she's in.

'Hong Kong. Then, I can take the exam and work in a hospital, if I learn Chinese, which I will, living there, really quickly,' Ivy continues after drawing a deep breath as if bracing herself.

'Chinese? Chinese!? It's not just Chinese!'

'I know mum, but—'

'Do you know how hard Cantonese is? After twenty years I can't speak their language here and they say Mandarin is easier. Easier! Twenty years and *xie-xie* and that's it!'

'But it's different. There you speak English, they speak English, you work for the English!'

'And thank God I do!'

They are both starting to raise their voices, as if they needed to shout to be heard over the distance. Neither is looking at the other's face on flat screens in front of them, they are shouting into the corners of the rooms they are in.

Later, Mary is hanging the batik sheet over the window in her room, its dark indigo blue swirls blocking out the glare from the neighbour's outside lights. They are always on late, come on early. She can hear the beeps from the washing machine outside the back of that house, the first load finished before she even gets up. She finds the television remote among the papers on the table, turns the lights out in the room but leaves the fan and the TV on, gets into bed in the flicker of the screen. She changes the channels for a while, skipping both the US reality TV and the teleserye on Pinoy TV and settling on the world news again. She should probably tell ma'am not to waste money each month on the Philippine channels that she never watches.

She stares at the television for a long time, the sound is off, but she has already seen the news earlier today so she knows what the images are about, even though she can't quite make out the headlines moving along the bottom of the screen. She thinks she can hear a faint ticking sound from the shelf on her right, but she's probably imagining it, or perhaps it is the watch. She holds her hand in front of the little yellow egg on the shelf, shielding it from the air current emitted by the fan. Is it still moving?

She takes the plastic egg off the shelf and gently gives it a shake. She twists the two parts of the container apart, putting the top part aside before pouring the contents of the lower part into her left hand. Eight little white teeth in her palm. Twelve swallowed or lost in the post or forgotten about, but eight are here with her. She closes her hand into a fist, looks at her own fingers, no ring, twists her wrist a little and puts the spiral her index finger and thumb make to her lips.

14. Cupcake

The neighbours are going away for Christmas. They come over to ask her to keep an eye on their house, and their maid. That's not quite how they phrase it, but that is what they mean. The maid is staying behind, in charge of the house and looking after the dog: they want to make sure the helper does not disappear. She is not sure whether this is a founded concern or not, and she does not ask, but of course she agrees to help. They get along well enough with the neighbours; they have nothing in common with them. They say hello and exchange pleasantries. Their attempts at further socialising have been examples of their differences. They invited the neighbours for dinner, just the four of them; the neighbours returned the invite, to a fancy-dress party. She is pretty sure neither couple enjoyed the experience much. But enjoyment is not what neighbours are for, they are for watching your house when you are away. Your house and your maid.

The first day after they leave, she sees nobody at all in the house. It is a Sunday, so it is the maid's day off. The dog is outside on her own. The mutt is a Singapore special, a puppy from a litter of strays, and the children have named her Cupcake. The dog looks sad and abandoned, and she worries. She hopes the maid will come back to feed her. Cupcake is an outside dog, mainly, although she sneaks into the house whenever she can. But now the doors are all closed, and the dog is stuck outside. She is not even sure where the dog is meant to sleep. It is still alone as night falls. She resolves to kill the maid when she comes back.

Her worries about the dog are unfounded. She hears someone in the bathroom the next morning, the patio door is a little ajar, and Cupcake seems happy and fed. If she kills the maid now, the dog will be abandoned, so she gives herself some time to observe and plan. The ideal day is the day before the neighbours come back. She is not entirely sure when that is, but it won't be long after the festivities are over. For the time being she can enjoy her first holidays in Singapore and prepare a murder.

Christmas in the tropics is odd. It doesn't quite feel right, despite her efforts getting a tree. After some investigation into the possibility of a real tree, she settles for a fake one. Real trees are not only expensive, and in bad environmental taste, but there are question marks over how long they can last in the heat and, the straw that breaks her camel's back, the water pot needs to be treated to prevent mosquito breeding.

The second phase of investigations revolves around where to get a good artificial Christmas tree. The answer seems to be the legendary Tangs on Orchard Road, a department store housed in a mock-Chinese building with red pillars and a layered roof of green enamelled tiles with their ends curling up. There is a decent selection of trees at Tangs, not cheap, but cheap is was not what she is after. She chooses a medium sized, fuller-needled one. The sales assistant tries to sell her scented sticks to hang in the tree, purportedly mimicking the smell of a real tree. He has her smell some testers. She feels like saying, 'you have obviously never smelled a real tree,' but she doesn't.

They decide that having a barbecue on Christmas day is the way to do yuletide in a hot climate. She wants to go out for a big brunch in one of the hotels, but he turns semi-traditional and insists they have Christmas lunch at home. He draws the line at the turkey, however, and they buy steaks and cold cuts and cheese. In the event, the heat at midday on Christmas day puts them off even barbecue steak, and they have cheeses and biscuits and ham and salami and champagne for lunch, the meal leaves them full and tipsy, and then, in the evening, they're hungover and in no mood for the barbecue. There isn't much to do but watch some films and nap. In between, she observes the maid and her routine.

The maid doesn't have much to do either. She gets up early, though she never walks the dog. She feeds it and herself. She has a shower. She does some cleaning, some tidying in the garden. She goes out. She comes back. Sometimes she is out for longer than a few hours, but mostly not. She has a shower. She goes to bed. It is a thoroughly dull routine. Even though the neighbours' maid must recognise her, they ignore one another, they never say hello. The few times she has been to the neighbour's house the maid has been working in the background, cleaning and tidying at a party, bringing out food and drinks, clearing away the dirty plates, glasses and rubbish. When she'd gone into the kitchen to ask for something – perhaps forks? – the maid had provided some without a word and not much eye contact. She hadn't made much eye contact herself, feeling that strange middle-class guilt at a domestic servant, at the same time as a little envy. She could have one if she wanted to. She knows she would happily adapt to one, and is almost dispirited at her own scruples. Her scruples about keeping a domestic servant are greater than those about killing someone.

Whenever she walks past the older shopping centre down the road (the newer malls don't have such low-grade shops) she glances at the maid outlets with curiosity and horror. Sometimes the maids sit inside, waiting to meet prospective employers. Sometimes they are ironing, displaying their skills. She is sure he has seen one with a baby doll, but she may have imagined it, heard the story from another outraged expat, read it in the paper. It disturbs her that they are on show like that, like puppies for sale, but it also amazes her that someone would simply come in off the street and browse for a maid. The maid shops advertise maids from a range of places: Philippines, Indonesia, Myanmar, Mizoram. She had to look up the last, it's a region of Northwest India, sandwiched between Bangladesh and Myanmar. She doesn't know why this region, in particular, is flagged up as a source of maids, but the internet indicates that they are cheap.

Every time she passes by the neighbours' house, she looks for the maid, a small woman, but larger than many other maids. She presumes she is Philippina, but having never spoken to her, nor to the many other maids she sees daily, she has no way of knowing if the stereotype is true. She sometimes hears maids talk to each other in what she assumes is Tagalog, but she could be wrong.

She spends some time looking at an online forum that appears when she searches for Mizoram and Google automatically suggests 'Mizoram maid.' It confirms all her stereotypes about maid-owners. Someone, in a post a few years old, asks if Mizoram maids are any good, as the going rate is only $350 a month for Mizoram and

Myanmar maids. A Philippine maid is nearer $500. Actually, it has gone up to $400 for Mizoram maids, the questioner is informed. Some other users share their bad experiences with Mizoram maids: scowling faces when taking orders, breaking things, eating too much, demanding specific brands of coffee. One complaint catches her eye: '3rd only stayed a week cos she did nothing except to sit in the middle of the kitchen floor, beat her chest and wail cos she was homesick. She also grumbled non-stop.' She tries to imagine a move to a new country, on her own, living in a stranger's house, expected to perform daily tasks in a particular way. It was difficult enough for her to move with her husband and dogs, to her own home. She too would be sitting in the middle of the kitchen floor, beating her chest and wailing because she was homesick. She did. She was.

She meets a woman with a beautiful dog on the beach. She is drawn to the power and grace of the woman's Rhodesian Ridgeback, and they start talking. The dog's name is Ronaldo, Susanna's two sons are avid football fans. Ronnie is sixty kilos of muscle and paws the size of saucers and forty-two perfectly white teeth and ears like newly cooked pancakes and all cuddles and slobber. After cooing over the dog, she finds out that the owner and she share the country they were brought up in. Upon discovering their this, they swap languages immediately, a sign of recognition. Her second first language feels rusty and strange in her mouth, but she perseveres, it is the code of admittance to a quickly formed club of foreign nationals abroad. The English lack the possibility of the exclusivity of this club because everyone speaks their language. Perhaps that is why they view speakers of other languages with such suspicion, wondering if they are being talked about. It always struck her as funny in London when the English voiced their concerns at being spoken of by foreigners on the tube. As if people had nothing better to talk about in their native tongues. Do the maids speak only of their employers in Tagalog? Susanna and she speak of Singapore, and maids.

She is a little surprised to learn that despite her Northern European upbringing, Susanna has a helper. The helper helps take the kids to school in the morning and helps take the dog out in the evening, meets up with the other maids in the condo complex and their families' dogs down at the shared gardens, and has a nice chat. She also helps with cleaning and cooking and shopping. Susanna and the maid have coffee every afternoon, after the kids are back from school, and discuss what needs to be bought for the evening meal. The helper gives Ronaldo a shower after he returns from a long walk with Susanna on the beach, to get rid of the sand and the salt in his fur because Ronaldo sleeps in between Susanna and her husband at night. The helper has a nice room on the lower floor of the house. A little on the small side perhaps, and no air conditioning of course, and Susanna felt bad about that at first. She considered putting the helper up in one of the spare guest rooms on the second floor of the house, but a friend had talked her out if it. They had made that mistake. Once the helper was on the same floor, they kept bumping into her. They were constantly reminded of her presence. Retreating to their bedroom felt less private when she was next door. They could hear her. She could hear them. The helper started feeling like an overdue guest. No, Susanna said, allowing the helper her space, her floor, is essential for keeping the relationship working. Despite the coffees, she is the helper, they, her employers.

The neighbours' maid is wearing a 'I heart SG' T-shirt. She has seen a lot of maids wearing them. She wonders if they are being ironic, voicing a little quiet underhand protest. So many women in 'I heart SG' T-shirts sweeping drives, taking out the rubbish, washing cars, walking dogs. This maid is cutting back some plants outside the neighbours' house. She smiles at the maid, and the maid half-smiles back, but only for a second. She doesn't recognise the maid. Is this a new maid since that fancy-dress party? Or does she not remember the face of the person that had served her? Do they actually all look the same to her, people of other races? She cringes. The maid is smaller than she recalls but probably strong. The maid's unsmiling face makes her think there is a fierce interior, she can imagine the woman kicking, screaming, punching, biting. There is a fire in the maid's eyes, a sort of despisement when she returns her gaze; a condescension even, mingled with pride. You will never know my life, it seems to say, so why even try smiling at me? Or maybe she is projecting it all. Maybe the maid is just bored and tired.

She walks past with the dogs. She presses the button on her blue plastic remote to open the gate and looks back at the maid. The woman has turned her back and is cutting plant stems with the scissors in her right hand, her left holding an ever-growing bunch of cuttings, until it is too large to hold and she puts it in the bin. The maid looks at her again when opening the bin lid, appears surprised. She turns away quickly; her own gate is open.

She imagines stabbing the maid in the shower, *Psycho* style. Before she can react and bite back. If she gains entry, it will be by the maid letting her in, and then there is no element of surprise. She has no ladder, although she could climb the fence, but that would be very visible and conspicuous. She could give the maid some poisoned food, but there is no guarantee she'd eat it, and she has no idea how much poison and what poison is needed to kill someone so that they don't just get sick. Then she'd be in trouble, although she could probably blame it on the ingredients. Poison herself and him a little and say we all got sick it must be the whatever I bought in wherever. The maid's situation, in the old-fashioned sense, her employment as a domestic worker, protects her. The house she resides in to clean and cook and tidy, is not a prison but a protective cage. But it also isolates and hides her. The maid is not part of the same society as she is. If only she can overpower the maid, she will be able to kill her. She needs a gun, or a poisoned dart or syringe of toxin or crossbow. All of this is insane. She cannot get those items, where would she even start, and it would leave a trail, make her a criminal. It would make her enter a world where she could be traced and tracked and labelled and unmasked. She needs to keep this simple.

After Christmas, when he goes back to work, she goes over to the neighbours' house after several cups of coffee in the morning. She takes some bug spray, a newly purchased butcher's knife, and a long T-shirt in a 7-11 plastic bag. She rings the bell and the maid, whose name she still doesn't know, comes to the gate. She says she is in need of some eggs and sugar, realising how clichéd and hollow and odd it sounds, with a 7-11 two minutes' walk away from the house and while she is clutching a 7-11 bag in her hands. The maid looks at her with surprise and an emotion she cannot read: suspicion or distrust or incomprehension or maybe disdain at her stupidity. The maid looks at her 7-11 bag.

'The shop has run out,' she says, with as much conviction as she can muster. 'Please can I come in,' she continues, hoping that her insistence and frankly, whiteness, will make the maid comply. The woman does, saying something curt and incomprehensible as she opens the small doorway in the gate and lets her in. The dog comes wagging its tail but shies away when she bends down to pat it. She doesn't wait for the maid to show her into the house but strides up purposefully. 'No eggs,' the maid says, following. She doesn't look at the maid but continues up the stairs leading to the patio from the drive, kicks off her sandals, and goes in through the open doors. 'You must have some sugar, though. A cup would be great, thank you very much.' The maid follows her in, across the floor of the sitting room, into the kitchen at the back of the house. She knows nothing of the layout of the rest of the house, she has only been here for a party, but she knows where the kitchen is.

She stops before she enters the kitchen. 'Yeah, so sugar...' she says, turning to the maid. The maid looks at her for a split second and says something that sounds like 'Yes, ma'am,' and walks past her into the kitchen. While the maid opens a cupboard with her back turned, she pulls out the bug spray and the knife. As the woman turns around with a bag of sugar, and opens her mouth to say something, she sprays her face for a good second or two. The maid screams – loudly – and drops the bag of sugar, which goes everywhere, and clutches at her face. She had worried that she would not be able to act quickly enough, but the woman's screams spur her into action, although her action is not very well thought out. She stabs the maid in the stomach, hard and quick. She withdraws the knife and keeps it in her hand. The maid starts hitting out, but she can't see much and is confused and in pain from the spray. She starts coughing herself too, from the cloud of bug spray spreading throughout the room. She backs off, realising that the maid being blinded her is her advantage. The woman continues to hit out with her arms to defend herself from her unseen enemy, still screaming but less loudly, struggling to breathe. The maid is bleeding from her stomach and her body starts bending forward from the shock and pain.

She moves aside and allows momentum to take the maid past her, and then she grabs the woman's hair and pulls her head backwards. The maid's arms shoot up clutching at the air, fingers bending like claws, getting more bent with each time she raises her arms, one after the other, up and down, until she is beating the air with her fists, as if she was boxing someone suspended from the ceiling. Meanwhile she slits the maid's throat with the knife, awkwardly reaching around her armpit, in a strange embrace. The first time she passes the knife across her neck it only cuts the windpipe, the maid's screams become gurgles and hisses. The second time, firmer now, she hits the artery and there is so much blood. The maid is weakening quickly, her boxing blows becoming smaller, shallower, until she is beating a very small opponent, and then none at all. The floor is covered in sugar and blood, becoming diluted with the piss running down the maid's leg. The woman becomes very heavy and slumps against her chest, and she falls onto the slippery floor with the body on top of her. The blood is still bubbling gently at the cut at the throat, but the maid is not moving anymore.

She extricates herself and goes to the sink and washes the knife very carefully with dishwashing liquid, rubbing it very thoroughly all over. She dries it and puts it in the rack of knives on the counter. Then she takes her clothes off and cleans herself with the tea towel and the washing up liquid. She rubs herself very clean. Once she is clean, except for her feet, she puts the T-shirt on and puts the bloodied clothes in the 7-11 plastic bag. She finds a large plastic bowl and fills it with water and washing up liquid. She steps over the body of the maid, and places the bowl outside of the sugar, blood, and piss mess. As she steps out of the coagulating, smelly, granulated paste, she steps into the bowl, holding the plastic bag and the tea towel in her right hand. She washes her feet thoroughly, dries them, and places the dirty tea towel in the plastic bag along with the clothes.

As she exits the kitchen the dog is there, looking at her and wagging its tail. She stares at it for a moment. Then she goes back into the kitchen to look for dog food. It is almost impossible to move around the room without stepping in blood now, the pool of gore is widening. The smell of blood and piss is strong, odours are so much more intense in this heat. She is surprised the dog is not trying to come into the kitchen. It must have been scolded for doing so in the past. She gives up looking for the dog food, she can't reach any cupboards without stepping in blood, then remembers there was another fridge and a kind of pantry at the back of the house – she got some beers from it at the party. It would make sense to keep the food for an outdoor dog outdoors.

She goes out the back door, the dog following her at a little distance, still wagging its tail. After a brief search of shelves and cupboards she finds a bag of dry dog food and a bowl. There is a small cup in the bag with the kibble, and she measures out two cups into the bowl. The dog is skipping from foot to foot, watching her as she does so. She puts the bowl down, holding her palm facing to the dog, saying 'wait.' The dog gingerly makes an attempt to get closer to the bowl, and she repeats 'wait' a little more curtly, holding her hand in front of the dog. The dog gets it and stops. It even sits down. She smiles and says, 'good girl, go on then,' and the dog looks at her a little uncertainly, and she has to repeat 'go on' and point at the bowl before it goes to the food. With a lowered head and still looking at her from the corners of its eyes so that the whites are showing like little crescent moons, Cupcake starts eating. Soon the food gets the dog's full attention.

She sits down on her haunches and watches the dog eat. She should leave, run away, but instead she adjusts her legs so that she can, not entirely with ease, place her feet flat on the floor. She sits there, crouching, like she has seen so many maids do on their day off in the city's open spaces, congregating in flocks, chatting in their birdlike language.

15. Dr James R Rogers

He knows his hair is too long, too thin to be too long, too grey and in need of a wash, probably. He knows he should shave, but he cannot, not again, not today. Let it grow. Let it grow, like the plants outside the window, constantly growing in the heat and the rain. There is no autumn here, no fallow time, no time of death and decay, and no regeneration either, just growth, overgrowth, like a cancer, he thinks, I sound like Werner Herzog, but my hair is thinning, no cancer of the hair. He puts on a newly washed shirt at least; he's picked a lot of them up from the cleaners just yesterday. Ironed and crisp, a soft shell to hide the ageing flesh within, a soft-shell crab, exoskeleton seemingly strong, but easily devoured, chewed, and swallowed in salted egg yolk coating. They are normal crabs, soft-shell crabs, just in the process of changing their armour, having shed and left the old one behind, vulnerable for a few days. But they look the same, yes, they look the part. How many metaphors? May as well mix them, an ever growing soft shell crab decaying in the mangroves of the swamp they say this place was before we came to teach them how to trade.

All narratives are lies, he thinks as he pours himself a coffee and lights a cigarette on the balcony. It's just a matter of finding the right time and place to tell them, to make them sound convincing and true. Normal people don't know what's true, that it doesn't exist, and it makes no difference how many books he reads and articles he writes, they will know no better. He wonders if his students remember, out there in real life. Do they understand or simply rehearse? Do they ever stop and think, in industry, what is a fact? is increased productivity always better? do I even exist? He knows *he* only exists because he swapped ponds many years ago, the big one for the small one, where no one knew he had no shell, where his size was big and where he started to rot. No, maybe the rot had set in before, the rot was there all along, a disease caught in the metropolis. No vaccine.

He stubs out his half-smoked cigarette, he's getting sweaty, time to go in before the shirt crumples, before the cookie crumbles. I am a crab, here are my claws. He takes a taxi to work, for the same reason, he tells himself. It isn't far, from his flat to his office, only a short walk really, the flat is virtually part of the campus, a condo built to house academics from abroad. He pays a fraction of the rent he would anywhere else in this city, and lives a few blocks away from the university, but it is still too far to walk to work in this heat in a clean shirt.

His mother died a few weeks ago, he was back in the home country then, cold and bleak and the rain drizzling from an incessantly grey sky. He took a taxi to the funeral; grief is best not shared on the bus. They hadn't spoken in years, she didn't speak for the last five, no narratives left in her ravaged brain. He saw some friends then, realising they were no longer friends, just parts of the narrative his own brain was still busy telling itself. No facts.

The taxi drops him not far from his building on campus, just a walk across the open courtyard, around the lawn, he gets his pass card out as soon as he is out of the taxi.

The office is cold and dry. He keeps his books here, the dehumidifier is always on and yet he can see the edges of the pages starting undulate ever so slightly, a little more yellow each day. The first years here he kept his books at home, until he had to consult a work long unread and it fell open, the brown stained pages sliding out of the binding. Had he imagined it or were the pages covered by microscopic dust, spores of some fungus eating through his library? He had to wash his hands after, and threw all the books away, started anew in his office. Maybe if he would keep himself in the office more he would decay more slowly, he thinks, as he makes a coffee using a small kettle and the one cup cafetiere he keeps in a drawer. He sits in his chair, swings it around to the left and reaches out to a row of folders on the bottom shelf behind him. He pulls out a binder full of papers in plastic sleeves, opens it, finds the right spot, and snaps the metal rings open. He takes out a sleeve and puts it on his desk behind him, shutting the folder and replacing it on the shelf. He swivels back on his chair and looks at the papers, covered in transparent plastic, on his desk. It is week three of term, and the lecture is on structuralism, as usual. He's given it many times, but he likes to have the papers there, in front of him at the pulpit. In case he forgets. In case his mind goes blank. It never has. Yet. He's never been speechless, never not known what to say. Except, of course, all the time.

He has time for another quick half-cigarette before the lecture. He hides at the back of the building in which both his office and the lecture theatre are housed. No smoking on campus, but he's not the only one. They greet each other with furtive glances, the smokers here by the loading bay, the workmen's entrance, the rubbish bins. He can feel sweat breaking out by the time he heads back in, welcomes the arctic blast of the lecture hall aircon. He does his thing, rattles off his piece, summarises Hegel's influence on literature and literary theory in fifty minutes. A potted history, an intro to ideas, a window onto debates. A lecture is only a taster, a starter, to whet their appetite for the main course, the reading, the research. How many will be tempted by today's menu? Then they have seminars and tutorials, where their own ideas can be tested and heard and discussed. That is the narrative, of course, the narrative of curious minds and independent thoughts. They're good at doing the reading, here. He's good at summarising the information, at drawing out the right answers, he thinks as he walks through the corridors of the building to the seminar room. He has a group, as do a couple of colleagues, splitting the cohort up into manageable sizes. It's about asking the right questions.

Does he have time for another half a fag? He escapes out, is late, the students are all seated and waiting when he enters the cool of the seminar room, relieved as the sticky film on his skin disappears in the dry, processed air.

He starts by going back to the beginning, to Saussure, to make sure they understand. To make sure the break is made in their mind. Word and thing. The sundering of which starts a revolution of thought, makes possible the thinking not simply of what makes us who we are but how we make ourselves. How the human experience is *structured* (and thus able to be *re*structured). It begins with the word and the thing parting company. Will they understand? Make the link? He always worries, although he needn't, not here. Back home, monolingual, a few students always remained unconvinced. He never learned Chinese. God knows he tried. Here he is the simpleton when it comes to comparative linguistics, even though his French is pretty good these days. Nevertheless. He is the conduit to extrapolation, text into theory. What the French do best.

He draws a river above a river, intersects the two with dotted lines. Amorphous thought and featureless sounds. As and Es and Ts and Rs and Os and Bs. He draws a tree. He writes 'tree.' He writes 'arbor.' He doesn't write 木. He did once, many years back. Looks like a tree but doesn't sound like a tree. Nowadays he stays away from Chinese characters, after having spent an hour being taught by his students about radicals and components and sound and sense. There had been no time left for Saussure, the founding father of structuralism. He imagines himself to be the serpent in the garden of language, offering the theoretical apple that will open his student's eyes to a knowledge they can't unsee: that what seems God-given shows itself as man-made. Or at least he hopes they will think about it for half a day, before cramming the facts, sitting the exam, and forgetting it all again.

'What does Saussure's idea of how language works mean for us as literature students?' He asks. 'What does it mean in terms of the way we view the written word?' He pauses briefly, ready to answer his own question like he does so often, although he tries not to. Pedagogy. But pedagogy can be so time consuming sometimes. Like talking about Chinese characters.

'It's no longer true.' A voice from the classroom, as he draws breath for the next sentence, so he stops, exhales, looks into the faces all pointed towards him like sunflowers in a small field. He walks across the front of the room and they follow him like the sun. Except when he speaks, when they all wilt into their notebooks. But he's not saying anything now. What else is there to say? That's it, really. In a nutshell.

He suddenly thinks of his mother again, here in the middle of class, her wordless face. Ravaged, diminished, reduced – the expressions that they used to categorise her, then. But she herself was without sounds, back in the river of amorphous thought. Perhaps not even that, no longer bound by arbitrary phonemes and ideas, she was finally free of the illusion of truth, existing without narrative and therefore existing in perhaps the truest sense possible for a human being. By losing her humanity, leaking slowly from that category into the surrounding world, becoming part of it. Her gaze out of the window of the nursing home, without judgement, immediate, true. Becoming world.

16. Academia

The metaphorical killing of her academic career. She has decided not to apply for that job. Nearly decided. Actually decided, she realises looking at the deadline, or was it next month? June, July – they sound and look the same, especially here in the tropics. Maybe there is still a chance to jump back on that horse she had decided to get off, at least for a while. For a while-forever, more likely. Perhaps, she thinks, she needs to kill a literature professor.

She has been considering the possibility of killing with a blunt object blow to the head for some time. Is it even possible? It happens all the time on screen. One clearly has to hit hard, but how hard is hard? If she wallops with all her might, will it kill someone? She tries to remember the scenes she's seen. Often the first blow is not deadly, at least in the more realistic dramas, but it renders unconscious or at least stuns to such an extent that repeated blows are not resisted, or not resisted enough, and the job can be finished. She knows who she wants to kill next. That man. The one that was helpful-not-helpful, in that awful self-important academic way. We're so busy, so busy. 'What? In your head?' she wants to scream. 'You're an academic for chrissake, have you not noticed how hard other people are working?' But she stops herself, because perhaps that is why she is a failed academic, because she has never worked out how to be busy.

The man had been mentioned to her by a fellow academic in London. Somebody equally busy-helpful but neglectful. She has started to become like them. Not doing the job properly. When she had started lecturing, she did the job thoroughly, well, on time. Like she had always done. In business it had earned her some respect, she could have gone far, made a great manager, somebody had once told her. But by then she had already decided to give up business and go become an academic. Was that seven years ago? Suddenly she thinks of that inspirational article, shared online, that proclaimed that it takes seven years to learn something new properly and so, the logic went, every seven years it is natural, right, obligatory, to change horses, so to speak, and learn something new. It had inspired her, for sure, a spur to get off that dying nag of working in an office she was on then. So now she was trying to figure out if it all worked out in sevens. Stopped working and did a PhD, but that was longer than seven years ago. Separate the doctorate time out. It took a little less than seven years but a bit more than the suggested three for her PhD, so somewhere in between, not bad.

But then what was going on? Was she half-way through the seven years of a half-hearted attempt at a post-doc academic career? No, she had been teaching for about seven years now, since before she'd got her doctorate. And she was good at it. (Perhaps you were allowed to keep going for more than seven years if you were good at something?) Ok, that worked. Seven years of trying to become an academic, a second rate teaching academic at least, and maybe now was the time to kill that horse. To get off it and shoot it dead. Hit it over the head with a shovel.

That fellow, whose name she was given in London. She emailed and he didn't reply. When she arrived in Singapore she emailed again, this time she got a reply, noises about meeting for a coffee. She felt encouraged until the follow up replies never came and there was no meeting. He gave her some other contacts though, and she tried to make other connections, but it's hard when you are not bound to an institution. They really have very little in common, her and the people she meets, except for tentatively a profession – but one, she soon realised, that means that each is obsessed with their own little bit of knowledge, in such a way that they always talk beside each other, never to each other, even though they pretend they do. She meets some new academics for lunch, they share some experiences of moving to Singapore, but as usual she feels inadequate when asked about her own work. The lack of it. Work that is the only work, research. Teaching never cuts that mustard, it isn't real work to them.

She is invited to a reading group on the theory of aesthetics. It is exciting to read the challenging texts, to meet people who share her interest. The man she's emailed turns up, too, so finally they met. He seems pleased, and she wonders why it had been so hard to have that coffee, then. Something about a mother in frail health back in the UK. Perhaps it was true. She tries to prise some logic out of that reading group. She tries to make them explain, decide on terminology, see the schema, but they don't speak that language. They never do. Everyone has their own ideas, their own jargon, and everyone else tries to connect in snatches, grab a word that makes sense, and then they all pretend it is dialogue.

At the reading group he tells her there is to be a job advertised at the institution, and that he thinks she should apply, even though it is a position she is not senior enough for. She is not quite sure why he says that, if he really means it or because he thinks he should be kind after being so elusive, or perhaps because they are just desperate for people to apply. She knows her CV is not up to scratch, she stopped doing proper research a while back now, and with that her employability recedes quickly into the past. It is hard to do research without institutional support she tells herself, when in fact she simply does not like it. She found it hard to do a PhD but she had done it, and she had enjoyed it. But afterwards it all seemed to become a mercenary exercise of research for publication's sake, a race, a chore, a job. She just can't muster up the enthusiasm, the introversion, the ego. The stuff she wants to research is either unpopular with the establishment or seems ridiculously self-engaged, or both. She teaches and she likes it, and she learns a lot from teaching the stuff she has researched. She learns more from having to explain it, make it digestible.

She has never quite understood how the academic world works. Her brain puts up a barrier when she hears terms like the research excellence framework. She can't make herself interested enough to find out what it really is or does or measures. She does not know which journals are valued at what scores or whatever. She wonders why she feels such antipathy towards this part of academia. Is it a fear of personal failure – if she figures out the measures, will she realise how short she comes up against them? Or is it truly some sort of sense of the wrongness of this kind of bureaucratic imposition on centres of learning and knowledge. She really struggles with the bureaucracy in Singapore educational institutions. Like everywhere in this place they seem to thrive on red tape. Maybe that is why she is getting slack in her work, all that form filling and box ticking. But show me a job that doesn't have its fair share of that. Perhaps the realisation of the extent of these people's love for procedure adds to the decision not to apply for that job, maybe it is that ever-present fear of failure, or maybe it is because she had found an alternative occupation.

She emails him and asks for a meeting, about the job. She is more forceful now about setting a place and time she has a reason to meet, she is not just looking for contacts. In the morning of the meeting she takes the dogs out; they go to the beach in search of stones. They walk up and down the East Coast Park looking for blunt objects of adequate heft to kill a man. It must be heavy enough to provide some momentum to the blow, but it can't be so big that she can't carry it in her handbag into someone's office. The dogs grow restless as she picks up debris and weighs it in her hands. Nothing here is up to the job. On the artificial beaches of Singapore there are no stones big enough, only imported sand and managed lawns. She goes home and after she has fed the dogs, she goes out onto the streets of the neighbourhood.

There are several construction sites around. There is always another house being built, even when you think there couldn't be space or demand for one. Suddenly one of the older houses is gone, just a pit in the earth. Those are the sites she peers into, not the ones nearly finished with the plastic film covering newly installed patio doors, but the dying embers of the old before they are extinguished entirely by breeze blocks and concrete and steel and weathered wood panelling.

She's in luck, one of the sites has progressed little over the last few months, is often left empty. Demolition started, but there seems to have been a snag, and building has never got going. The hoardings around what is now a square of gravel and hardcore are not very well secured, and she gets in easily. No one is there. She stands in the square, in the middle of the dust and rubble, the heat starting to beat down in earnest now. It resembles a boxing ring, with fences on four sides like ropes, and her in the middle, the only fighter. She gazes up at a merciless sky, but soon has to look down again, it's too bright, too empty, too hot. She glances down at her feet already covered in building site dust. She takes a few steps around, aimlessly, poking things with her feet, picking them up and dropping them again. All stone-like objects, really bits of broken concrete, and they are either too light, or too big, or just an awkward shape.

She finds a piece of metal, a bit of concrete armature red brown with rust, with a pattern of welts along two sides. It is slightly bent, about thirty centimetres long. She picks it up and weighs it in her hand. Perhaps. It has the advantage of being much more manoeuvrable and easier to wield than a stone, a branch-shaped object for hands evolved to climb trees. It makes her think of her father's strange edict that she should not roll up papers and carry them as if they were sticks. They had been in a museum, where they always give you more paper than you need, and she always rolled it up. It was a throwback to her wild ancestry, her father said, to hands that want to grasp branches. A civilized person, a human, should make the effort to carry the paper as paper, not as a branch. Denying ourselves our brutish nature, even in this small instance, was somehow necessary to him. Is the way you carry paper a sign of your good breeding, of familial eugenics good enough to erase residual animal nature from the bloodline? No, that was not it, it didn't really sound like her father. It was about mind over matter, another sign of intelligence above average. When most people would roll their paper up into a comfortable branchlike tube, those who had the insight into their true natures, who recognised the beast within, would be able to resist, and so to transcend.

She weighs the metal rod in her hand: it is nice and warm, it has a rough texture that aids a firm grip, a steel branch with the regular bark of industrial manufacture. She lets her arm drop to her side, holding the short, bent pole in a forehand grip. It feels safe and natural. It adds to her stature somehow, this tool she has appropriated for herself. She swings it in the air. It extends her arm, part of her intention. She has no choice anymore; this is going to have to be the thing.

She goes home smiling, swinging her treasure by her side. The heat of the day has started, and not many people are about. The few that see her may wonder, but only briefly before going about their business, hurrying to where they have to go, quick out of the cruel sun. At home she cleans the metal rod in the kitchen sink with water and soap. It colours the water a rusty red as it turns a dark grey itself. She doesn't want to wash the rust off, just the dust. She lays it outside in the sun to dry, like some kind of fruit she has picked and wants to preserve.

She has a shower, washing the concrete powder off her feet and hands. She puts on her somewhat smarter attire. Here in the tropics her uniform in London, jeans and t-shirt and a hoodie, finished off by trainers or wellies, has been replaced by a skirt, t-shirt or sleeveless top and Birkenstock sandals. She's found some three-quarter length jeggings (isn't that what they are called, thicker than leggings, stretchier than jeans?). A pair of black jeggings with a white shirt, not even really a shirt as it only has a button-less opening at the neck and no collar. A pair of black ballet pumps, and she looks decent enough. She takes the bright yellow leather bag that her mother once bought her. It is just big enough for an A4 size folder containing a CV and an iron rod of about thirty centimetres length with a bend in it. She places her implement in the bag along with keys and wallet and phone. She encourages the dogs into the garden for a pee, calls them in again and closes the patio doors. She finds her favourite sunglasses, that he bought for her birthday two years ago, and the car-keys and shouts to the dogs to stay and be good and goes out the door that locks by itself behind her.

She gets into the hot car, turns the ignition, switches the air conditioning to full, sets Google maps on her phone to take her to the University, and places it on the magnetic holder at the corner of the windscreen. She puts some music on Spotify, plugging the phone into the stereo to charge and play. She presses the button on the remote for the gates to swing open, puts the car into drive and goes, pausing to shut the gate behind her. While on their road, unable to speed up, the aircon is weak, and the car hot, but as she gets onto the main road and is able to accelerate the cool kicks in and she has to turn the switch down a notch and point the nozzles away from her. Always too hot or too cold.

The traffic is light, a testament to the success of the prohibitive pricing of car ownership. The roads are spotless, the driving bad. For a country so keen on rules, drivers are surprisingly uninhibited in their interpretation of the highway code. She shouts and swears more driving here than back home. In London traffic is aggressive, but there is some communication, some acknowledgement. Here there is no eye-contact, no nods or waves. It seems so terribly rude to someone used to British roads. And counterproductive. They are all trying to get somewhere as quickly and smoothly as possible. Not allowing people out at junctions, cutting people up, overtaking on the inside, none of this is going to help any of them in the long run. For a culture where collectivity is meant to be key, there is a lot of selfish behaviour on the roads. It is the isolation of the car, she thinks. Asia is non-confrontational, deferential face-to-face, but when your face is protected by steel and glass, then you can look away and ignore the rest. Although she has heard about cases of road-rage, sparked by rude gestures. She shouts behind the closed windows of her now very cool car.

The National University of Singapore is a campus university, but since most of Singapore looks like a campus it simply seems another part of town, perhaps a little smarter than some, less commercial than others. Here are the high-rise blocks, the planned walkways, the shops and food outlets. Convenient, provided, integrated. It is cool, shaded, and air conditioned away from the teeming life of the tropics. Plants are managed, tamed, delineated or delineating, nature in the service of architecture; fallen leaves, runaway roots, wayward branches are swept, cut, pruned. Those exist only in the margins now, where the stray dogs live.

She parks in the underground carpark, and a lift takes her directly to the centre of this artificial village of learning. She skirts the softly shaped lawn, surrounded by high-rises, none of them square, and no harsh doors, no abrupt inside-outside boundaries. Curved galleries, enclosed spaces leading to semi-enclosed spaces, leading to shaded areas, leading out onto the lawn with the cold blue sky above that is actually so hot. She squints at it now, skirting the exposed central area. Outside is too hot, inside is too cold, but where she's walking is just right, perhaps a legacy of more primitive living, in houses with shade and breeze rather than glass and glaring heat that needs to be sucked up and spat out by humming machines. Stilts and open walls are echoed in the concrete pillars and mezzanines of the campus complex.

She finds the right building and enters the cold lobby, waits for another lift – so many lifts. She gets off at the 4th floor. His office is here somewhere. Offices are numbered along with classrooms; she walks around for a while trying to find the right direction to reach the room that she is after. Corridors open into atriums and then narrow again behind glass doors. Daylight and electric light take turns to illuminate white walls, doors, corners, and floors. She has to go back on herself several times, having reached dead ends. Her bag is over her shoulder, under her arm, feeling heavy.

She finds the office and knocks. She enters as the voice within bids her. He is not an attractive man, one of those ageing white men to whom twenty years in the tropics have not been kind. White frizzy hair too long, too thin. Reddened veined skin, damaged by sun or alcohol or both. An awful patterned shirt. A limp handshake and evasive eye-contact. She finds him instantly repulsive. She wants to take out her blunt metal implement from her yellow leather bag, fling the bag aside and raise the washed gun metal grey but reddening already from rust rod with both her hands above her head, and bring it down on his skull. Hitting him where the slightly flaky skin of his inflamed forehead meets the receding hairline of nicotine yellowed grey hairs. Crack his head open like an egg and see the crimson flow out, a living, livid red liquid from inside this decaying exterior. The truest, most alive thing about him. His blood. From inside his head where all those academic thoughts live, that he brings out through his mouth in hesitant yet authoritative phrases about aesthetics and philosophy.

Softly spoken, but aware of his position of superiority to others in any room – the professor. His students deferential, his colleagues admiring, even in disagreement. The publication list, the tenure, the funded research project, it all shores up every sentence he says, even when it makes no sense.

His blood makes perfect sense. It appears quickly after the first blow, above those pale blue eyes washed out by the sun, rimmed red and moist. She raises the rod again and brings it down again, even as he is lifting his arms in defence. She doesn't give him time to finish the manoeuvre, it remains a vague gesture of resignation as she hits him anew. His arms drop as if in exasperation, as if he's waving away someone's preposterous argument. There is more blood now, running down the sides of his nose. She raises the rod a third time, hits him a third time, takes a step towards him as she does, and she can feel something crunch under the rod, his skull giving way. He staggers backwards, bumping against the desk and chair, his back finally hitting the bookcase at the end of the room. She lifts the rod off his head, some blood and skin and hair stuck to it, and lowers it by her side.

She wants to hit him again and again, but she is afraid of seeing the mess that would make of his head. He already has a large wound just above his forehead. The idea of a crushed skull, nose, face, broken eye-sockets, and brains spilling out suddenly frightens her. She watches him crumple and slide down towards the floor, against the books. He is still looking at her, so she swings the rod at the right side of his head, from over her right shoulder, as if hitting a baseball. It connects and makes another hole in his head. The force of her blow pushes him over to one side. He's almost lying on the floor now, on his side, against the shelves. He has stopped moving. He's too close to the books for her to swing at him comfortably. She uses her foot to push him away and turn him over, face down. She stands over his lower back, one leg one either side of him. She brings the rod down on the back of his head as hard as she can. She swings her arms from far above her head and she bends her knees at the end of the arc to give her more power. Again, and again. The brittle wisps of his hair turn from yellow-white to red-brown, his skull cracks and crumbles, and there is some soft pinky-grey matter appearing. She doesn't mind seeing it from this angle, without a face it is just the flesh of an overripe fruit broken open as it fell off the tree. Blood and hair and brains splash and splatter over the books on the shelves, the floor, his back, her front, her arms, her face.

What a coward. If she were to kill him, she should make herself look into his disintegrating face, at least. She feels disappointed in herself, the same way she does when she thinks about all the meat she eats without having ever witnessed the death of the animals she consumes, the hypocrisy of the modern carnivore. But she isn't killing him. She cannot kill him here in his office. It is a preposterous idea. She sits down and they talk about the job she doesn't want.

17. Wine Fridge

They find they have to buy a wine fridge. Expat life creates new and tawdry necessities. Sure, moving to a new country, a new climate, means readjusting your life materially. But she finds that so many of their new needs are articles of comfort she would usually consider reserved for the rich. And they are rich, in the grand scheme of things. Living in Asia had has made her more aware of how close to the extreme on the global spectrum between privilege and misery she is. She knew before, of course, saw the graphs and charts and percentages in the Economist, but here, even in one of the wealthiest nations of the continent, inequality is more open. It is less frowned upon. Europe has a way of smoothing over socioeconomic gaps. Here there is less pretence.

They went to Western Australia for five days on a tour of the Margaret River wine region. There were possibilities to buy wine in bulk at better prices than those that made her weep in the shops in Singapore. Being rich enough to buy wine more cheaply leads to its own problems. An investment in a cooler suddenly seems a necessity. The more you have the more you need. Then the pain of trying to find out which one is the best buy: European or Japanese? Single or dualtemperature zone? How many bottles? She gets antsy and impatient. She finds spending time on this kind of research annoying. She wants to understand the need to spend one's money wisely, but she is not sure she does. The way she can relate to these choices is by time, the currency she has the most of. She makes virtually no money, but time is her own. Time is worth something to her, the way money is not. On the other hand, if she were to buy something which proved a waste of time, this would be more annoying than the waste of time spent in choosing it. Hence, some insight into purchases is necessary. Things that do not work the way they are meant to are an overwhelming waste of time.

She tries to take a step back, to let him do the thinking he needs for this purchase. It doesn't really matter to her; it seems to matter to him. She would not have chosen to make the purchase he makes, but she is fine with it, it will stop all this deliberation. He settles for a slightly more expensive model, but a display unit, reduced in price. Dual zone, 32 bottles, Japanese made. When they had bought their first house, they bought a fridge made by Samsung. It broke after a mere two or three years. He vowed never to buy a home appliance made by a mobile phone manufacturer again. Their next fridge was made by Liebherr, who also make heavy earth moving equipment for the mining industry. Gigantic diggers and trucks. That fridge was still going after many years. She has no idea what Kadeka make apart from wine fridges.

They settle the bill and arrange delivery. The wine fridge comes a few days later, she is home to accept the consignment, but some visitors are arriving that day and she doesn't have time to get it running. She has the delivery men dump it in the middle of the living room as they have not decided where it will go yet. The men want to install it for her, of course, they alwasy do here, but she says no, so they show her where the electrical cable is located (at the back of the fridge) indicating that it needs to be plugged into an electrical socket (at the corner of the room). She nods and yeses and sighs. Just leave it there, it will be dealt with. They give her the instruction booklet, and then depart.

Busy with visitors, it is a few days before they pay any attention to the appliance. He and a friend from cooler climes inspect the fridge, chatting about the strange need for a wine fridge. They cannot talk about the wine fridge without irony. Then they realise that it is defective, even without turning the damn thing on. The door seal isn't flush, the rubber does not touch all the way around – the door must be warped. She knew buying a display unit was a mistake, trying to save money, she would not have done that. It is under warranty of course, but now she will have to spend time getting it fixed.

The stopwatch measuring the time wasted starts with the phone calls that need to be made. To the seller, then to the service company.

Somebody is always going to look into it and call her back. Days pass, another call, another wait, more days. There is never any dispute that the fridge is in warranty, but neither is there any assurance that it will be fixed or replaced. She has never quite got used to the evasive, noncommittal way of business here. Not no, but not yes, either. We will do our best. To her ears it sounds like an excuse for not delivering, the beginning of a let-down. Really it is more of a get-out clause, an unwillingness to make false promises. In the West such promises come hard and fast, and they make you feel safe. Then you feel let down. Here you are just constantly unsure. She does not like feeling unsure. She wants things sorted and done, now. If there is a solution, then why not implement it at once and be done with it? If there is a problem, face it and figure out what to do next. Waiting is the worst.

Finally, she manages to get an appointment with an engineer who will come to her house and assess the issue. No promises as to whether it will be rectified or not, but it will certainly be looked at. As per usual she is given a two-hour window in which to expect the engineer. Her life seems measured out in two-hour windows for various deliveries and services. She would quite like a helper (not maid) to help with that, the constant waiting around. It is not that she goes anywhere much, but being tied down, expecting the doorbell to ring, is inconvenient, frustrating. You can't pop to the shops or take a shower or have nap. She is often asleep when they come. She gets up and staggers to the gate-opening buttons in the lounge. There are creases on her face from the pillow. Her skirt hastily pulled on, and askew. She grunts and mumbles to the postman, groceryman, dogfoodwoman. For the pest company and air conditioning engineers, she has to be a bit more compos mentis, as they stay a while. With deliveries she often just falls back onto the sofa or into bed again.

For the Kadeka engineer she has to be awake, to show and explain. The engineer is not what she expected. What did she expect? A cardboard cut-out fridge engineer in a dark blue t-shirt and dark blue work trousers? The man who arrives is older, smaller. He has a limp and a cane and comes with a small roller suitcase for his tools. He has unkempt grey hair. An 'uncle,' she thinks. She likes the man immediately; he is soft-spoken and kind.

She shows him the fridge, still in the middle of the living room, which seems to take him by surprise. He asks where they plan to place it, he seems perturbed by the fact that it has not been installed. She is more keen to have it fixed than plugged in, so she mentions it will go in the back, in the utility room – the maid's room, she has to clarify.

The engineer looks around the large living room.

'Ah, but this fridge is to display wine, with glass door. You want to place it here, near the dining table.'

'Yes, but there's no space here,' she replies, keen to get him back onto the issue of repairing the cooler.

'You have nice wine, you want to show it to your guests,' he insists.

'Also more air, more cool, here.'

'You think it will function better here, sure' she humours him, 'but only if the door is closing properly.'

'Ok, I will fix,' he gets the hint. 'Then I will install, move to where you want, no problem.'

He works away at the fridge; she hides in her office. She turns the aircon on for him in the living room. They almost never use it, this parade piece of a living room, with high ceilings and exposed beams and heritage Peranakan-style tiles. She has seen tiles like that in Joo Chiat, these are probably reproductions, but the landlady is keen they be careful when cleaning the floor, not to use too much cleaning liquid. No need, there is little use of those tiles except as a thoroughfare between rooms and front door and patio. Their furniture from London fits remarkably well in the room. Against one wall, a modern style oak sideboard from Denmark with rounded edges, facing it, the sofa and flanking the rug between these, a leather recliner, and a classic IKEA Poäng rocking chair. All in brown-grey tones. To the side the retro teak veneer table and 80s steel tube and wicker chairs she had found on eBay. A small bookcase, another small sideboard, both in light, unvarnished oak, by the door, and a standing lamp in a corner completed the room's furniture. It looks good, but it feels soulless. The dogs hate it: the girl rarely stops in the room, the old boy just guards the patio door if it is open and a bed is laid for him on the floor. As far as she knows the dogs have never been on the sofa in the living room, even though they frequently used it in London. The room grows uncomfortably hot on sunny days. The high roof, which to European eyes promises the coolness of circulating air, is, without any insulation from the roof-tiles heating up during the day, a giant radiator. On top of that, the acoustics are bad. Initially they place the TV on the large sideboard in front of the sofa, but whenever they try to watch it the people on the screen seem to mumble. No matter how loud they turn the volume up, in that large space the sound is somehow dispersed and distorted. After ten months of not watching TV in the living room but using a laptop in bed, they realise their folly and move the TV. Now they use the room even less, it is simply too spacious for sitting in, just the two of them. You feel exposed, lost. It is as if there is too much air above them. It doesn't feel like shelter. Like the dogs, some primitive instinct urges them to find a place more contained, easier to guard. The only time they ever use the lounge is when they have guests. It is great for parties. They never have any parties.

The engineer finishes and demonstrates to her how the door closes tight now. She is pleased.

'Now I install it, to test if it works,' he says.

She wants him to plug it in where it is, but he is insistent. He points to the corner by the front door where the smaller sideboard stands.

'Maybe here?' he suggests. She shakes her head; it is too close to the door. He looks across the room, to the corner diagonally opposite, next to the big sideboard, 'what about there?' They have considered that corner, but it will disturb the symmetry of the sideboard against the wall with the whitewashed exposed brickwork.

'No, it won't look good in here,' she tries to explain.

'But if you have nice wines, expensive wines, you want to show them off, no?' he urges. No, she doesn't, but she does not know how to explain that to him, she doesn't want to explain, and he probably doesn't want to hear the explanation. To her sensibilities, putting the wine fridge in a place where guests can see it from the dining table, would be to 'show off.' Of course, she wants her guests, at least some of her guests, to know that she drinks good wines. Not necessarily the most expensive of wines, but not cheap either. A considered choice. To communicate this choice requires subtlety. It is part of a good show-off not to be a show-off. To show off one's tact and modesty at the same time as showing off one's good choice in wines, that is the trick. To make your guests admire the wine they were served, without feeling they had been prompted to admire it.

No, I want it in the back,' she pulls the curt card of the service-buyer. He doesn't argue and gets his small trolley, puts the fridge on it, then rolls it through the dry kitchen and the wet kitchen to the small maid's room at the back. She tries to figure out why he cares so much. Surely whether she displays her fancy wine to her friends or not means nothing to him. She understands why a few weeks later.

The engineer installs the fridge and sets it at very low temperatures. Six for white wine and fifteen for red. He stays a while to see if it is cooling down. It is. He tells her the fridge should be down to the required temperature in an hour or so, and if it is not, to give the service company a call again. The fridge struggles to get down to temperature within the hour, and to stay there, but it does a good enough job. She doesn't want to waste any more time on it. They go on holiday and come back. The weather gets hotter. When she goes to get a bottle of wine from the fridge one evening, she sees the two indicators showing 31 degrees. No cold upper zone for white wine, no cool lower zone for red and chocolate. The fridge has broken again.

She calls the shop and the service company again. They should never have bought a display item. They had saved money but are wasting her time. How much money is her time worth? At this rate certainly more than the few hundred dollars they had saved on the fridge. She gets another two-hour window, she waits, the engineer comes again. Same unassuming man, but no cane. His limp seems to have got a little better. He still carries his tools in a rolling suitcase. She had turned the fridge off after discovering that it did not function. For some reason she decided to turn it back on in the morning. It now started cooling again. Should she cancel the engineer? She asked him for his thoughts.

'No keep him,' was his texted answer. So she is duly at home, awake in the allotted time. She feels a little silly explaining to the engineer.

'So yesterday it didn't work at all. I switched it off. This morning I thought I would turn it on again... And now it works, but please could you have a...'

'Did you switch it on again yesterday?' he asks.

'No...' she hesitates, would it not be typical if this was a switch-it-off-and-on-again solution? The golden rule, always try turning the damn thing on and off, she hadn't realised it related to large appliances too. She will scream if that was that and he went on his way again.

'But it was not working *at all* yesterday...' she repeats, feebly.

'Does get hot here?' he asks, and she knows he is implying this was a bad location. 'More air in the living-room, cooler.'

She can't remember if he mentioned heat as a factor in the placement of the fridge the last time he was there. She can't understand why he wouldn't have. His worry about the warmth of the room is more logical than his worry about her displaying her choice of wine. After all, that is his job, to ensure optimal functioning conditions for the fridge. What wines she stores and the ease of her guests' appraisal of those wines is none of his business. She felt this constant slippage of meaning and intention here in Singapore. A reluctance to say what was required for the intended outcome. Instead, a secondary narrative is constructed in order to elicit the same outcome, but by a roundabout way. A way that is less direct diktat, a way that will make the person needing to conform or take action in order to reach the goal, feel better about doing so. Except, of course, if the secondary narrative does not appeal to the intended recipient and the whole thing backfires. She does not want to show off her wines. His suggestion that she do so had the opposite effect, making it obvious to her that the wine fridge should, in fact, not be placed in the living room, but out of sight at the back. Where it was hotter. Had the engineer explained that the fridge needed to be placed in as cool a location as possible, she would have been more likely to accede. She won't move the wine fridge now; she has wasted too much time already.

'Well, yes it gets hot here. But it gets hot *everywhere*, the whole house is hot!' She nearly continues, 'that's why I need a goddamn wine fridge!'

'Please can you just check it...'

'OK, I check.'

She offers him a glass of cold water. As opposed to the living room where he worked last time, the small room at the back has no air conditioning. It is pretty hot in there. She retreats to her cool office.

He works for a long time. He goes to his van to get more tools. He asks for a cloth.

'Compressor clogged up, need to empty all the oil. Messy,' he explains. The floor of the little room is strewn with parts, and there is a blow-torch at hand, she notes as she provides him with an old towel. Some serious fixing. Whatever was wrong with the fridge clearly requires more than an off-on solution. She feels vindicated. And dismayed. They really shouldn't have got a display unit, broken before they even got it home. What other faults lurk inside that cooling cupboard, and how many two-hour windows of her life will it demand? All for some wine at the right temperature. The required temperature. Two-hour windows of her privileged life for more privilege. Wonderful.

Over an hour later, the engineer is finished. The fridge is cooling. But the room is still hot. He shows her the part of the compressor that he has exchanged and which was the culprit. Some kind of inlet, a filter. She nods. She has a basic understanding of how a fridge works, probably better than most, in fact. She knows what a compressor is and why it is in a fridge and what it compresses, but at that moment, she really does not care.

'Is there sun in this room in the morning or afternoon?' The engineer asks. Back to the issue of heat. She is not sure, actually. She thinks about it.

'Erm... morning.' But the house is a one-storey bungalow, in a city situated one degree north of the equator. The sun beats on its roof all day long. She really does not want to have this discussion. She can sense that he will try to persuade her to move the fridge. He does.

'The wine cooler must work very hard when it is hot. Now you have warranty it is ok, but when warranty runs out... This job is $300,' he indicates his tools. He is just a kind uncle, with grey unkempt hair, concerned about her getting the best out of her purchase.

She cuts him short. 'It does get quite warm in here, I will take your suggestions into consideration.' She is not moving the fridge.

He relents. Again, she is instructed to check how well the fridge cools. If it does not reach the temperatures it is set to, to call him again. She sincerely hopes she won't have to.

The fridge never reaches the temperature set. The days are getting really hot now, and when there is drying laundry in the utility room, or the tumble dryer is on, it becomes very warm indeed. A goddam tumble dryer. It is hot, but humid. She is sure they are spending more energy here on cooling and drying than they ever did in the UK on heating and drying. Cooling the wines, cooling the rooms. Airconned air is too dry, and she often wakes with a sore throat. She is told she needs a humidifier. If its sunny the clothes dry quickly, but if it rains the air inside is too humid in the non-airconditioned back room. She is told she needs a de-humidifier. She uses her old tumble dryer, brought from the UK. She was clear that she wanted it here, remembering the musty smell she couldn't get out of clothes when she had been backpacking in South East Asia fifteen years ago. Her books are slowly acquiring yellow spots, their pages becoming warped and wavy, curling like hair. Is there a being growing on them? she wonders. A fungus, or a rot? Is it cheaper to run a dehumidifier or air conditioning in every room with books in? And the oil paintings. They will crack, she expects, at some point. Like they have been told to expect the wooden furniture will once they take it back to a drier, cooler climate. Back to civilization. They hang the two paintings most precious to them, the ones by her father, in the bedroom. It is the most often air conditioned room. But not all the time. The books can't go in there. Most of them don't even fit in her office. A lot are still packed away, in a little storeroom. She does not want to think of what is happening to those books in the dark of their boxes. What creatures are colonising them, nibbling their edges? She has never felt so at odds with nature as here, not just the critters, but the very air.

Things decay at a faster pace in the tropics, decompose, dissolve. Even sturdy leather shoes don't last, the animal skins seem to disintegrate somehow. Fabric shoes mould, the glue of the soles gives up its stick, rubber dries and cracks. There is an invisible army of micro-organisms hell-bent on returning the man-made world to dirt. They are not even properly animals, things that are something between living beings and the air. It is all a sliding scale here, from inanimate to scurrying and alive: the damp, the mould, the mushrooms, the weevils, the cockroaches. A common ailment among expats is mycoplasma infection, a kind of mild pneumonia caused by one of the most primitive forms of bacteria, a form of life so basic it lacks a cell wall, thought to be the result of reductive evolution. An organism that has gone back in time, simplifying itself. Its very simplicity makes it resistant to antibiotics. Parasitic, it lives in the respiratory tract of humans. Spread and outbreaks of disease caused by the bacterium 'tends to occur within groups of people in close and prolonged proximity, including schools, institutions, military bases, and households,' she reads online. Expats. Like their books and paintings and shoes and clothes they are worked upon by the forces of this climate. But there is no exemption for the locals. They are as much at war with the air of Singapore as its transient population. The Singaporeans she meets are some of the people most averse to coming into contact with their own climate. Using aircon, spraying houses and streets, bleaching clothes, taking more antibiotics than any nation she has come across. Many prefer, if they are given a choice, to live in a flat than a house, high up, away from the invasive nature of the region.

A city of skyscrapers risen from the jungle. The fishing village transformed into metropolis. Now little remains of either village or jungle. The process has been one of many steps and interventions. The copious vegetation of the city state is no virgin forest. At its wildest it is land that nature has reclaimed from many years of plantation and cultivation. But most of it is tamed into shapes and lawns, an imitation of the primeval forest – with improvements. As you drive from the airport to the city you pass lush umbrella shaped trees and ever-purple bougainvilleas. Neither are native to the region. With the foresight of those creating a new nation, the city planners planted South American rain trees to protect the motorway from heavy downpours, and the pretty bushes from the same continent to welcome visitors with their spectacular hue, which goes on and on along the route to town.

She wonders if they did the same to the villagers of that fishing port, now no longer. Moved the people into high rise flats, while naming the areas they left behind Chinatown, Little India, the Arab Quarter. Planting exotic species in manicured gardens, a recreated jungle. Restoring Chinese shophouse facades fronting new air conditioned malls. But critters survive, and so do people. Evolve and colonise new habitats, create new cultures. In the wet markets and food courts and void decks of HDB estates, there is what remains of the fishing village, adapted to the metropolitan suburb. Cleaner and more ordered, but with the old flavours still lingering. An amalgam of the noise and the heat and the cool and the steel. Bug spray is wielded in the corners of flats, the hawker centres are cleaned in strict rotation. Nonetheless, there are cockroaches and there is damp, the mess of life can't be fumigated away so easily.

.

18. Kenny

The hotel room looks like any other business hotel room, but smaller. There's a bed, a bathroom, a phone, a TV. But the sides of the bed nearly touch the walls, the bedside table seems like a normal bedside table sawed in half, the TV is pretty much above your feet if you lie in bed and watch, and to be honest there is nowhere else to watch it from but bed. The bathroom has a toilet and shower and sink so close together you could multitask of a morning. Shit, shower and shave, he thinks. Works for me, he thinks, he can't stand too long on that leg when it rains. He sits on the bed and massages his knee. It's not bad today, it has been hot and dry for a long time, one of the longest stretches without significant rainfall in Singapore on record. He's been following the weather reports carefully. Some days have reached thirty-six or thirty-seven degrees Celsius. He has never known it to be so dry and hot for so many weeks. Singapore is blessed with mild weather, warm but not too hot, wet and verdant but no typhoons, no snowstorms, no droughts and no earthquakes and no tsunamis. Well, now they are talking about a drought, but it's hardly the Sahara and his leg has been nearly pain free for almost a month, so he's not going to complain.

Kenny turns the TV on and starts flicking through the channels. Stops at a football match, checks who is playing, watches a while. She is taking a long time today. They have rooms down the road, but he doesn't like it there. The red light bothers his eyes, he can see the glow through the curtains, even at the back, although that is probably from across the street. It's dingy as hell too, it makes him sick. These days he doesn't even go there anymore, he just calls ahead and gives them a name and a time and the room number in the hotel. Like Chinese takeaway in the American films, he thinks, why do they always have to give a number? Three-five-six, egg fried rice. Number five, Sabine.

He's been seeing Sabine for a while know. He likes her a lot. She's not too chatty but doesn't mind speaking about her life, when he asks. And she tells the truth. The other ones kept on lying, making up stories, telling him about lives they could not possibly have had or why would they be there, with him. About Sydney and Bangkok and Tokyo and Dubai, even New York. He has no interest in these places. He went to Johor Bahru once, and to KL. They seemed much like Singapore, but dirtier. He was worried about the hawker stalls, chose to eat in restaurants only, to avoid food poisoning. It cost him a fortune. That was many years ago, he has chosen to stay home since then. When his mother died, he managed to hold on to the flat, even though he wasn't yet twenty-one (but very nearly) and he probably didn't quite fit in with the EIP and SPR quotas and he wasn't the one who should have inherited it. But his brother had no interest in it, chose to move away, so he ended up with the flat, a decent size for a single man. He should probably have downsized, but he was fond of the place.

He leans over the end of the bed to where his little roller suitcase is stood. He can reach it without getting off the bed. He unzips it half open and pulls out a blue plastic bag, top tied in a knot. He undoes the knot, and rolls the sides of the bag down, making a little blue basket, which he places on the bedside table to his left. The bag is full of longan fruits.

He goes back to watching the TV again, takes one of the small yellowish balls out of the bag and bites down on it lightly, just to feel the thin shell crack. Then he squeezes it between his finger and thumb, a translucent orb emerging, a dark seed just visible at its centre. He doesn't look at it, pops it in his mouth. Chews for a few moments, spits the seed out into his hand still holding the empty skin. Without taking his eyes of the TV he places the skin and seed on the bedside table and takes another fruit from the bag.

19. Wee-Min

The hotel reception looks like any other business hotel reception, but simpler. The glass doors, the wood veneer front desk, the faux-leather armchairs, the fake orchids, the bowl with mints, they are all in place, and Wee-Min, in a white shirt and black skirt and jacket, is standing there behind the desk.

Wee-Min has just started her shift, the late evening to early morning one, and her body says it is time to go to sleep, she is tidying the papers and receipts behind the desk to stay awake. There is a small desk under the front desk, with a computer, a phone, a copier-printer and a stack of plastic trays with papers in. And a dark grey box that is the key card encoder. The phone rings.

'Perfume Rose Hotel,' she says into the receiver, in a tone that manages to be sing-song and entirely devoid of mirth at the same time. 'Yes, sir. Certainly. One moment please... Putting you through. Have a nice day.'

'Evening,' she adds, remembering the time, but she has already clicked the voice on the other end away.

A man comes through the doors. He is wearing a crumpled linen shirt and shorts. Sandals on his feet. He looks hot and sweaty, his light brown hair, although cropped short, is sticking to his neck and forehead. He walks past the front desk and to the lift, presses the call button. He is holding a rolled-up newspaper which he taps against his leg as he waits for the lift. Once, he turns around and looks at her, and kind of smiles. She smiles.

'Good night, sir.'

He doesn't reply. The lift doors opens and he goes in, doesn't look at her again even though he has to turn her way to press the button for his floor. The doors close. There is not much interaction with guests on this shift, in these days of key-cards. Wee-Min imagines that in the past they had to ask for keys, hung neatly in rows behind the desk, and for messages, perhaps. Now the machine spits out the white card as she punches in the room number. Many guests drop the card in a bowl as they leave, having settled the bill before they even start their stay. Efficiency and ease, cleanliness and discretion are the buzzwords by which the Perfume hotels are run. Affordable efficiency and ease, value cleanliness and economy discretion. Everything you need, and not much else. Working here pays her bills and not much else. She takes some documents from the top tray of the tray stack on the desk under the desk and looks at them briefly, then turns the printer-copier on and feeds them into it. The copier spits the documents out again from one slot and copies from another. She puts the originals and the copies in the tray above the one she got the papers from. She sighs.

She looks up and sees a man exiting the front doors, he must have come out of the lift just now, when she wasn't looking, but she doesn't recall hearing the 'bing.' Perhaps he took the stairs? She feels a gust of hot air as he holds the doors open a little too long, as if he was hesitating. He is wearing a dark suit and a tie, although she must be imagining the tie as he is turned away from her. His hair is jet black and neatly combed. He exits and the doors swing shut, and the cool of the aircon envelops her again. She feels goosebumps on her arms for a moment and looks around for something to do. She is still standing, she doesn't want to sit down, in case she'll fall asleep. She bends down underneath the desk under the desk and gets her phone out of her bag. She is not allowed to use it during work hours, but she is so very bored. She places it on the desk under the desk so that it looks like she may just be perusing some papers as she stands looking down at it, but if you look carefully you'll see the faint glow illuminating her face.

She doesn't know how long she has been browsing Facebook, occasionally smiling at something to herself; she forgets where she is and she picks up the smartphone to type faster with two thumbs, commenting on something to her friends. She looks up and sees a girl standing in the middle of the reception area. She hadn't noticed anyone come in, she puts the phone down a little too quickly, it drops on the floor with a little thud. The girl doesn't seem to notice.

'Good evening, miss. Can I help you?' Wee-Min says, but she already knows that she can't. The other receptionists tend to ignore these girls, but she always makes a point of treating them like anyone else that comes into the hotel. After all they might be. How do they know? She may be a wife, a colleague, a friend.

They know.

The girl shakes her head ever so slightly, as if she is shaking a bad thought off.

'No thank you,' she mumbles.

She takes a few steps towards the lift, presses the call button. The lift is already there, and the doors open immediately. She walks inside and Wee-Min can see her smooth her hair in the mirror just before the doors close behind her.

20. Sabine

The hotel lift looks like any other business hotel lift. Sabine sees herself enter the small space in the mirrors on the back wall. She tries not to look at herself, but there is little else to see. She manages hardly to look at her white high heel sandals, or her legs, brown, a little too round. It is harder not to look at the short white sleeveless polyester dress she is wearing, but she avoids the bulge of her hips, only glances at the stomach, almost flat, but not quite. Her shoulders, slumped a little, she pretty much misses, ignores the somewhat too thick arms, but the round face is there, just in front of her. Pink lipstick. She sees her own small hand touch her forehead, just by the hairline. Involuntarily, she feels the bump, it is still sore but she can't see it, even when she leans closer to the mirror and looks for it. Her friend has done wonders with the make-up. The lift doors close behind her, but the lift doesn't move. She suddenly realises she hasn't pressed any buttons. She also realises she's been holding her breath against the pain. She drops her hand, exhales and turns around, presses number 5. The lift jolts, rises, stops. Doors slide open.

Sabine exits the lift, turns left and walks down the carpeted corridor. Beige and dark lilac. Doors on both sides, lights above, at even intervals. Beige carpet, dark lilac stripe. Beige walls, dark lilac doors. The fluorescent lights are placed in the ceiling right between the doors, then comes a section of the passage without doors and lights, then a pair of doors and a light again. Door door light, a little darker, door door light. She walks past four pairs of doors, underneath four fluorescent lights. At the fifth pair she stops, turns to her left again, facing dark lilac plywood. A metal number reads 517. She knocks.

He opens the door, smiling. He is almost as short as her. His hair is greying and a little messy. He has glasses on, and looks like a kindly uncle as he says, 'Come in. Come in. Please.'

He steps aside for her as she enters the room. There is not much space in there. He has to move along the bed to let her in.

'Sit. Sit.'

Sabine sits on the bed. He stands next to her, very close. There isn't really anywhere else to stand. The TV above his head is on, small figures are moving against a bright green background.

'Do you want a drink? Cold? Or I make you tea?'

She shakes her head. 'No thank you.'

He looks at her for a second then turns around to the small bedside table, as if he has just remembered something.

'Some fruit! I have longan.' He turns back to her with an open plastic bag half full of small yellow-brown balls. She sees a pile of discarded peels and stones on the table behind him. 'Please. Very sweet. Good for relaxing.' He holds the bag very close to her face, so she takes a fruit.

The logan is in her hand, in her lap, as he kisses her. She feels the rough skin of the fruit, rolls it between her thumb and fingers, back and forth. She starts kissing him back, then stops.

'Something wrong,' he says, more like a statement than a question.

'No,' she says.

He is quiet and looks at her for a while. He doesn't try to kiss her again.

'Trouble at home.' Another statement. 'Tell me.'

'No, everything is fine.' She looks at the longan fruit in her hand. Keeps rolling it. She inhales, pauses. 'I'm going to go away.'

'Where? Home?' This time he is asking.

'No. Away.'

He sits next to her, close, close enough to kiss, so when his fist hits the side of her head, she is not sure what has happened at first. There is a black flash at the back of her vision, and she is lying down on her side on the bed.

'No,' he says. 'Not away.'

Sabine lifts herself up on her elbow. She is still holding the longan in her hand, which she instinctively lifts to feel her temple, where the make-up was covering the bruise so well. It looks like she is holding the fruit up to him. When he punches her in the jaw, she can't help but drop it, she can see it rolling away on the hotel floor, but it doesn't go very far. The room is so small. She sees the longan come to a standstill by the wall before she falls back onto the bed. She sees the ceiling, it looks newly painted, there are no cracks. She sees his face, it is almost as big as the ceiling, there is just a thin, square halo of white around his hair. It's unkempt, and there are streaks of grey in it, and he punches her again. She sees flashes of black and flashes of light, even though she closes her eyes, even though she covers her face with her hands. She doesn't feel any pain, she knows it will come later, like it did last time when she got into the lift and saw herself in the mirror.

21. Sharp Shards

After a week or two she realises she has to call the engineer again. Another two hours of her life will disappear, this is no longer funny. She knows what he is going to say. She knows what is going to happen.

The day of the appointment begins cooler, a thundery shower passes, dropping temperatures outside and inside. She is always amazed at how much difference some evaporation makes. An endothermic reaction extracting heat from and releasing water into the atmosphere. But for a cooling effect to be felt there must be enough rain to lower the temperature sufficiently not to be cancelled out by the increase in humidity. Luckily, even short showers are copious here. For a while everything is fresh. She opens windows and doors to feel a little air inside. Real cold air. It doesn't last long and eventually the heat returns; it always wins.

When the engineer arrives it is starting to get hot again, even though the morning of rain has allowed the fridge to come close to the temperature required. She has to explain again about working and not working and now and before. They stand in the doorway between the dry kitchen and the utility room, looking at the wine cooler, displaying its 8 and its 16. The sun is beating on the roof, coming through the window in the wet kitchen, making beads of sweat appear on the engineer's forehead – and hers too, she realises, wiping her brow. It is a cue for what she knows he will say. She doesn't want him to say it again, she knows the damn fridge is in the wrong place. She was going to ask him just to check it, to make sure that there is nothing else wrong, as he said himself, it is still within warranty, better make sure now.

'Is that washing machine?' he asks, noticing the tumble dryer in the corner.

'No,' she has to confess 'it's a dryer.' She has placed the wine fridge in a room that is not only without air conditioning, but next to an appliance that generates heat. The little room is like a pressure cooker of heat. She envisions the room full of buzzing hot molecules, bursting. No more space. But there is no limit on temperature in the room, it can just get hotter, the fridge adding to the total heat. Why doesn't it just make it hotter in the room, leaving her wines nice and cool inside? Presumably some part of the fridge is limiting the rate of heat exchange. The compressor or the amount of gas, or the length of the tubes and pipes in there, something is defeated by this infernal heat. She, using the ingenuity of mankind, is trying to bring order, to divide space into hotter and colder. Keep things fresh, dry, preserved, long lasting. But nothing lasts. The goddam cucumbers rot in days here, even in the fridge. The more you try to chill the wine the more you heat the room. Until the fridge breaks. And it all tends back to the same temperature. The heat death of the universe is taking place right here in her utility room.

She feels her chest constrict, she can sense her own demise there, within her, her heart decaying with each beat, her body rotting from the inside, with every cell renewal a step closer to collapse. An endothermic organism generating internal heat, struggling on, blind cells shifting energy around, until one day some part of her, the pump or the piping, will give out. She looks at the engineer. Why is he bothering. Why does he care about her fridge? How can he go on living, tinkering with humanity's pointless devices? The vanity of it all is staggering.

There is a large frying pan on the drying rack above the sink in the wet kitchen, right next to the doorway where she is standing. The engineer is facing her, she can see his mouth open, hear the inhalation of breath, the oxygen exchange in his body producing more heat, some of it of coming out of him, hot air, she knows what he will say. She looks at him, and slowly reaches for the pan. She weighs it in her hand, it is satisfyingly heavy. When she bought it the lady at the check-out had commented about its weight. 'Heavy. Good. Best pan, heavy pan.' It's a kind of wok-frying pan hybrid, flat bottomed but with curved edges. Non-stick. Good for stir fries as well as shallow frying and even deep frying, she supposes, although she has never tried. Deep frying at home seems frivolously unhealthy.

She swings the pan, aiming to hit the engineer in the side of the head, but there is not enough room to swing, the pan catches on the drying rack, there is an almighty bang, and then a crash that seems to go on forever, as cutlery and several plates tumble to the tiled floor. There are shards everywhere, in little star-burst patterns around the impact site of each bit of crockery. The engineer just stands there, his kind uncle face with the grey hair in need of a cut looking at her. He removes his reading glasses. She adjusts her stance. She grabs the pan handle with both hands, lifts it, and brings it down on the engineer's head, looking straight into his soft eyes. They close just before the pan hits him in the forehead.

Unexpectedly he is still standing. Just standing there with his eyes closed, his arms by his sides, and the reading glasses slowly slide between his fingers and thumb and fall to the floor with a quiet, hollow 'thack'. They don't break. They are plastic. All of a sudden, everything is very quiet. It is very hot. The lower zone temperature indicator on the wine fridge changes from 16 to 17. She crouches down and without taking her eyes off the small, quiet figure in front of her, gathers some of the pieces from the floor around her. The large white dinner plates shatter in sharp cake-slice shaped fragments, she knows, because she has broken many of them. She is always breaking plates; she always has been clumsy. After this they must be down to very few, she will have to order some more from Macy's, international shipping, she's never seen those plates for sale in Singapore.

She gathers the shards to her chest like a bunch of sharp flowers and stands up. One by one she drives them into the fridge engineer's chest. The force of the first one pushes him against the back door. With each subsequent one he slides down, until he is sitting propped up against the door when she stabs him with the fifth and last ceramic slice. They are all in his upper chest, protruding from his grey shirt like little white flags with dark red auras spreading around them. She hasn't pushed the pieces very deep into him, their sharp edges hurt her hands. His shirtfront looks like it was made with a Marimekko fabric.

He still hasn't opened his eyes or said anything or even made much noise, apart from some burst sighs each time she stabbed him. She realises that her hands are bleeding and the engineer is still alive. For the first time since hitting him in the head with the frying pan she takes her eyes off his face. She turns around and steps back into the wet kitchen and surveys the contents of the drying rack, now all in the sink or on the floor. An almighty mess. Her gaze wanders over the metallic objects. She picks and choses, rejects forks, spoons and potato peelers. Pauses over the chef's knife, finally picks the large, heavy, ergonomically handled bread knife.

She walks over to the slumped man at the back of her utility room and grabs him by his bushy grey hair. She starts cutting his neck with the bread knife. Because of her stance and the way he is lying, she does it at a diagonal across his throat. The serrated edges of the bread knife rattle against the ridges and cartilage of his larynx. She can't quite seem to get through it, all she is achieving is to shred the skin on his neck. She never was very good at cutting bread. He would always complain that she mangled the loaf, creating uneven, ugly slices, impossible to fit in the toaster. The bread knife was a bad idea, driven by a concern about style over practicality. The engineer's messy hair is slipping from her grip, some of it coming off in her hand, his body leaning towards one side, sliding down onto the floor, forcing her to lean ever more awkwardly. She stops sawing away at his throat, and instead pushes him down fully on the floor. She kneels beside him, pausing for a moment, before raising the knife with both hands and bringing it down where she estimates his heart is, in between those white flags with widening red circles around them. He lets out a little whimper. She gets up abruptly and runs to the sink in the kitchen and throws up.

She has never been faced with a dead body in her home before. This is something new. Like the mould spores and ants, it has invaded her house. She needs pest control, but how do you kill death? Can you eradicate murder? What spray is there to remove a dead body? Bleach, she needs bleach. There is some in the little bathroom that is the 'en-suite' to the maid's room, and where her part-time cleaner stores the tools and chemicals of her trade.

The cleaner. The cleaner is coming tomorrow. She cannot leave the dead engineer for the cleaner. She starts by taking all her clothes off and cleaning herself. Since half of the tiny bathroom is filled with mops and buckets and cleaning liquids, she leaves the door open into the utility room as she showers and, when she has finished rinsing herself, she starts showering down everything in reach. She stands there, naked and dripping wet, showering the floor, the tumble dryer, the wine fridge, and the dead body of the engineer. The water and blood runs into the drain in a corner of the room, and slowly, very slowly, turns less red, more pink, paler and paler until it runs almost clear.

She feels cold. Water evaporates and steals heat from the atmosphere. The dial on the fridge has ticked down to 16 again. She finds a small towel in the bathroom and dries herself, then puts it on the floor just outside the door of the utility room and steps on it to dry her feet. She walks to her bedroom and puts on some clothes: pants, bra, a sleeveless top and a skirt. Same outfit as before, same outfit as always, except not stained by blood. She grabs the keys to the house that are on the island worktop in the dry kitchen, fetches her handbag from the study, checks that her wallet and her sunglasses are in it, and goes out of the front door onto the porch. She puts her sandals and her sunglasses on and presses the button on the key fob to open the gate.

She walks to the end of the road and then left and to the little Indian mom and pop shop that has everything. She loves going into that shop, likes just looking at all the potentially useful stuff they have. Milk and crackers, tinned vegetables and shower gel, toys, bust firming cream and envelopes, washing powder and light bulbs, bleach and bin bags. She buys bleach and bin bags. A spring clean, yes, she smiles at the unsmiling shop owner; he doesn't say anything, but she feels exposed. She says 'wait,' and grabs some other items she does not need, like milk and a toothbrush, and brings them back to the counter, too, and pays for it all.

She walks back home, taking her sandals off on the porch and dumping her handbag, her sunglasses and her keys on the dining room table.

The dogs have awoken from their slumber now and are curious. She lets them go out into the garden but not into the kitchen. She gives them some treats, as usual: a venison rib for the old guy, he settles on the grass with it, and then she walks around the house throwing dried lamb lung cubes for the girl to chase and hides a few more to sniff out. She sits on the patio chair while the old boy finishes his bone, and the girl finds and eats all the little titbits. She gets up, calls their names and walks around the house with them both again, encouraging the old hound to have a pee. When he's done, she walks back to the patio door and ushers the dogs into her study. She replenishes their water bowl, turns the aircon up a little, and closes the door as she walks back to the kitchen.

She puts BBC Radio 4 on. It's too early in the day in the United Kingdom for regular programmes, so all she gets is World Service. Listening to the news bulletin she unrolls the bin bags she has just bought and separates a few out. She cuts along the sides and the bottoms of each bag making them into large plastic sheets. From the cupboard in the dry kitchen, she fetches a roll of duct tape and goes back to the utility room.

The water on the floor has dried a little, it doesn't take long in this heat. The room is very humid and smells of blood and something like piss or shit or both but not quite. The dead engineer is lying alongside the wall, neatly. She lays three plastic bag sheets on the floor next to the body, overlapping. They are a bit on the thin side so she lays another layer on top. She is about to roll the body, when she realises she has to take the knife and the shards of plates out of his chest first. How has she not thought of this before? Apprehensive at first, she slides the knife out, and then carelessly yanks all the pieces of porcelain out of the engineer's chest. She puts them all in the sink in the wet kitchen. Then she rolls the body over onto the bags. It's heavy, but not heavier than it looks. It is about as heavy as it looks, she concludes with relief. The engineer was quite a small man. She has some trouble with his arms and legs, flopping and flailing. It would have been easier to push rather than to pull him over, but as he is lying against the far wall, she has no choice. Concentrating on levering the solid sections of his body, shoulders and hips, she manages to turn him over. She adjusts his limbs, settling arms closer to the torso, legs together, head straight. He is now lying face down in the middle of the small room on a sheet made of six black plastic bin bags. She adjusts the plastic sheet underneath the body, straightening out any bits that have snagged.

She goes back to the dry kitchen, drying her feet on the towel in the doorway, and cuts up more bin bags. She comes back and covers the body with another two overlapping layers of six bin bag sheets in total. She wraps the lower layers of bags around the sides of the body, folding the edges of the upper layers in, over the back, and tapes five strips of duct tape across the corpse, from side to side, securing the plastic bags. Five strips: one on the head, one across the shoulders, one at waist height, one by the thighs and one around the ankles. It's so hot and she's sweating. She must be dripping sweat on the bags, the body. She realises that there must be fingerprints all over, and sweat and hair, too. However much she would try, she'll never be able to prevent her DNA contaminating the body. She is kneeling next to the body. She sits back. She feels an enormous lump in her chest. For the first time she is feeling quite uncomfortable, now her adrenaline levels have plummeted. She feels sick and tired. She starts crying, sobbing into her hands. This, *this*, is not what she expected. Not what she wanted.

She heaves a sigh. Nothing to be done. She gets up and goes to cut up some more bin bags, returning to the body with another twelve sheets. She puts six of them in two layers between the wall and the body and rolls it over again. It is easier this time, as he is neatly wrapped and doesn't snag anywhere. She covers the body with another two layers of plastic and tapes them up, folding the edges over as before, but staggering the strips of tape between the previous ones. One strip at the neck, one at the chest, and one by the knees. Then she tapes across the bottom of the feet and on top of the head, folding the four layers of bags as neatly as she can, the way she wraps Christmas presents. Pressing the edges down, making pleats on the sides, folding the bottom edge up and over. Securing with some tape.

The engineer is now a neat parcel, wrapped in black plastic and duct tape. She is not satisfied that the parcel is secure enough, however, so she starts again. She goes into the dry kitchen and measures out six bin bags. Cuts them up along one side and the bottom. Takes them through to the wet kitchen to the utility room and spreads them in two layers of three overlapping bin bag sheets, next to the parcel. She rolls the body over onto the sheets, folds the edges, and tapes across in five places. Head, shoulders, waist, knees, ankles. She goes back to the dry kitchen again. Measures out bags. Cuts open. Spreads between the body and the wall. Rolls back over. Folds edges. Tapes three strips: neck, chest, thighs. Then head and feet, edges like a present.

By the time she has finished the shipping forecast is on: the start of Radio 4 programming in the UK. She feels calm. The body is now neatly packaged in twelve layers of bin bag sheets secured with sixteen strips of duct tape across and eight or ten smaller pieces of tape at the head and feet. It is back next to the wall. It's a little wet, so she wipes it down, first with a wet cloth with some cleaning liquid on, then with a towel, trying to get it as dry as possible, soaking water from all the creases in the plastic.

She takes a bucket and mop from the small bathroom and fills it with water and floor cleaning liquid. She mops the floor carefully, first with a wet mop then with a wrung-out one. While she waits for the floor to dry, she drinks a glass of cold water. She goes to the study and fetches her laptop, places it at the edge of the island in the dry kitchen, where the barstools are, and opens the lid. She types in Geylang into the search engine, and clicks on maps, then 'satellite.' She zooms in, drags the map left and right. Zooms out. She opens another tab in the browser and types in 'Geylang brothels.' She spends some time reading various web pages. She is curious and angry. Disgusted and resigned. There is a whole other world of hard-working individuals which she knows next to nothing about. At best she is a tourist, at worst a gawker, a voyeur, a peeping tom. More hidden than the domestic workers, these women, for they seem to be mostly women, are the hardest working of them all. The ones whose work is the hardest. Who work harder than even the Anglo bosses, or Chinese family fathers or Indian IT analysts or construction workers or Philippino maids, but who are not part of any cultural orientation narrative, except perhaps in passing. Yes, prostitution is legal, tolerated in certain areas. Geylang. You can go have a look at the big bright red numbers that distinguish the brothels form ordinary houses in the lorongs, the alleys, south of Geylang road.

She had heard of several new residents in Singapore who had gone for the tour, the gawp. The hidden world is the one the most on display if you know where to look. A little bit of free titillation. Looking is free, right? Or can a prostitute charge for a look? But how else is she going to advertise her wares, if she doesn't go on display? Part of the business, keeping a display copy for the customers to browse, except here you always buy the shop-soiled goods too. There is no new, shiny exemplar, brought out of the drawer from behind the counter. You can pretend she's a virgin, its only twenty-five 'til nine, but buying sex is not like buying a new TV. Or wine fridge.

Of course, she doesn't actually know, she has no frames of reference for this, except her own body. Perhaps buying sex is like getting a haircut. Selling sex is like cutting hair. A service, for a bodily need. One customer's haircut is neither more nor less, and has no impact on the next, except perhaps for increased skill and dexterity. She cut his hair once, on the beach of a South Pacific island. They sat in the shallow lagoon, in the shade of a palm tree, and she used the scissors on the penknife he had given her as a birthday gift. The result was atrocious. Even without the gentle waves rocking them as they sat in the soft sand, it was never going to be an even haircut. She tried the method she had seen her father use when he cut his own hair. One finger's breadth all over.

His thick curls fell into the sea and washed away, along with a coconut that fell off a palm tree. They joked about witnessing coconut reproduction in action, coconut sex taking place slowly over time and space. Left on his head was an uneven stubble – her finger seemed to be of variable size. It didn't matter, they laughed and made love in the lagoon. She was a little worried some strange tropical fish would inhabit their private parts. She can imagine neither cutting hair nor selling sex for a living.

She goes back to the utility room; the floor is dry now. She rolls the black plastic package over once more and wipes it down again, it is still a little wet on that side. She notices the engineer's reading glasses in a corner, so picks them up and folds them. Taking the scissors, she makes a hole in the plastic bag wrapping on the body. She stuffs the glasses in and tapes the opening shut. She mops the place in which the body-parcel was lying, next to the wall, and then pours out the dirty water from the bucket into the drain outside, fills the bucket with clean water and washes the mop out. She empties the bucket again, wrings the mop as much as she can and puts the bucket and mop back into the small bathroom at the back of the utility room.

She returns to the dry kitchen and to scanning the satellite images. She can't find what she is looking for. Instead, she sees the name of a hotel she stayed in a long time ago; later on the same trip as the haircut in the pacific lagoon. They passed through Singapore, backpackers on a shoestring. She does not remember of being aware that they stayed in the red-light district then. They had been taken there by the taxi driver, coming from the airport. A high-rise with minuscule rooms, he had thought it soul-less but she had found it refreshingly clean and well appointed (en-suite, TV, aircon) after the rustic accommodations of their previous destinations.

She had been persuaded that they should move to an area with more character the following night, and they had gone to a guesthouse in the Arab quarter. The room was on the second floor of an old shop house. She was horrified. The bathroom was shared, with no western toilet, and the floorboards in the bedroom had big gaps between them. She could see down onto the bottom floor shop, and the men that had stared at them when they arrived. She sat on the bed and cried until he took her back to the soulless hotel in Geylang.

On the satellite image the hotel casts a shadow behind it, creating a dark oblong behind the houses on the parallel street. It looks like a car park. This is the kind of place she is looking for. It is getting towards late afternoon, and she needs to do something about that black plastic Christmas parcel at the back of the house. She thinks a while. There is no way to get rid of it but to put it in the car and drive it off somewhere. There is no way of putting it in the car without simply taking it outside and lifting it in. She cannot hide it or disguise it in any way. The only thing she can do is wait for the dark, but he will be coming home, and, besides, an illuminated scene will be easier to spot, while a deliberately darkened one will surely be more suspicious. She decides to simply do it in broad daylight, minding her own business, as if it is the most normal thing in the world.

She drags the body through the house by the legs. It is dry and does not leave a trail. It catches a little on the threshold between the wet and dry kitchen, but the one between the dry kitchen and the living room is flush and it slides right over. She is glad she has packaged it in many layers. She stops at the front door, puts the body down, goes out and opens the car boot. She kicks a few pairs of shoes littering the porch out of the way as she returns to the door, drags the body out. The head bumps down the small step from the front door to the porch floor, and then again down the step from the porch to drive.

The car has the lowest boot she has ever seen on an estate car, and no lip. They decided to buy this car, a Honda Airwave – a model they had never seen or heard of before –because of this very feature. The old boy was getting older and had arthritis in his hip and his wrists. Jumping in and out of the car was only likely to get more and more difficult for him, although for now they were successful in keeping the degeneration of his joints at bay with monthly injections of cartrophen. It was strange drug she did not understand fully. She always wanted to understand how medicines worked, even in just a general way. Cartrophen – pentosan polysulfate – was used for bladder issues in humans, and arthritis in animals. She guesses it has to do with linings. Some efficacy in the treatment of Creutzfeldt–Jakob disease has also been shown, apparently. How linings relate to this she doesn't know, and it bothers her. The drug had proved very effective in treating the dog's arthritis. But the warmer climate had helped too, both by warming up his joints and by slowing him down. He rarely exerted himself these days. However, it was clear that slowly, inexorably, he would find it harder and harder to jump into the boot of the car in the morning when they were off for their walks at the beach or Gardens by the Bay East. Eventually she'd have to help him in, even lift him in. It was easier said than done with a thirty-kilo dog with very long legs. They did have a ramp, but it was a lot of bother getting it in and out of the car and to set up, and the dog hated it.

She briefly considers if the ramp could come in handy now. The body must be at least twice as heavy as the dog, although more compact. Unfortunately, the ramp has a kind of non-slip, sand-paper-like covering. She could not drag the parcel up the ramp without ripping the plastic to shreds, in several layers. She'll have to lift it. She is happy she's been working out, doing weights in the gym. Her legs are a lot stronger than they used to be. She may not be able to lift the body in one go, it is too long, but she can do it in two. She drags the body so that it lies parallel to the edge of the boot. She removes the dogs' cushions from the boot onto the driveway. She lifts the feet into the car first, they are light and take no effort, placing the body with its lower legs at a ninety-degree angle to its thighs, and its thighs at a ninety-degree angle to its torso. The body is still bendy enough. Then she heaves the rest of it into the boot by squatting down and placing her arms around the torso, from the sides, like lifting a large sack of dog food. It is heavy, as she lifts it up, she has to quickly place a knee under its back to stop herself from dropping the thing. She pushes it up the last bit with her knee and hands, almost rolling it over the edge of the boot. The head hits the taillights. She has to shift herself somewhat to the left and push the pelvis of the body into the boot first. Its knees are now hitting the back of the back seats, but the boot is big enough to accommodate two large dogs. Or a small man in a foetal position. The head and shoulders are still out, so she shuffles to the right, drags the chest out a little, holding it in place with her right knee, and folds the head towards the chest. She then pushes the top part of the body into the boot. It doesn't look too uncomfortable, she thinks, while wondering if any of the neighbours have seen her. It is still early enough for the heat to be intense, and nobody is about. She realises how much she is sweating, and how thirsty she is. She closes the boot and goes inside to have another glass of water. She needs to pee.

The drive to Lorong 20 Geylang takes less than ten minutes. She sets the satnav on her phone mainly to get an idea of which roads are one-way and which are two-way. It is almost impossible to drive anywhere in Singapore without encountering a one-way system. Wrong turns always end up as long circumnavigations. It doesn't actually matter to her now, as she may as well scope out the area and she is in no hurry, but she wants to be in control. She wonders if the entry to the car park she has seen in the satellite image is from Lorong 20 or the neighbouring Lorong 18. Lorong 19 is somewhere else, north of Geylang Road. South of Geylang Road the lanes are even numbered, north, odd. They are numbered consecutively starting from the Kallang river end of Geylang. A couple of early numbered lorongs have been swallowed up by the Stadium development in Kallang, some have become bigger thoroughfares, but most of the lorongs are still there, up until 40 and 41, by the Geylang river. They are not particularly narrow or alley-like, as she'd imagined. A lorong in the red-light district sounded like something narrow and dark, but the afternoon sun was beating down on two lane asphalt. Flanking the lane at the Guillemard Road end are two rows of small one-storey houses with awnings shading concrete drives, some open to the road, some with gates. Most houses have large signs with numbers on them, or have big numbers painted on gateposts. Most numbers, but not all, are red. Although she's read about the brothels, she is still taken aback by their brashness. But it makes sense, here in this ordered city of commerce, to have clear signage. Further along the lane towards the Geylang road end the small houses are replaced by concrete multi-storey buildings. Hotels. One of which is the Parfume Rose Hotel, in which she stayed many years ago. She has no recollection of the brothels and their numbers. She must have just thought they were very keen on making sure people got the right house-number in

Singapore. No confusion.

The lorong is busier than she expected, and she realises there are prominent CCTV cameras everywhere, on the house fronts as well as on street itself. As she drives along, she realises her plan is most likely no plan at all, but she still wants to try the car park. There are several signs for parking lots, for different hotels, as well as for on-street parking, payable by coupon, 50c per half an hour. She had read advice for potential johns on a forum she came across on the net earlier, to pay for at least an hour and a half, as the traffic police check the road frequently, and you don't want a ticket stating your location sent home. But parking is free after 5pm, the website added, should you wish to save some money. She presumes the transactions happen by the hour, and the extra thirty minutes on the parking coupon is for choosing, negotiating, washing your dick and paying?

There are two hotels on the road, 15Hotel and Perfume Hotel. The first one looks distinctly seedy, but she is surprised at the business-like feel to the Perfume Rose Hotel. Maybe it hadn't been such a bad choice to stay in after all. Maybe it was simply a cheap hotel. Close to dining and entertainment. Although the brothels are technically separate and streetwalkers are not allowed, she presumes the hotels must get their fair share of the sex trade. She misses the entrance to the car park and finds herself at the end of the lorong, at the crossing with Geylang road. She has to turn left into the busy traffic, and then left again into Lorong 18. She sees something that looks like the entrance to a parking lot and steers into it, but it turns out to belong to different building and is rather small. She has to make a five-point turn to get out. But she can see into the hotel parking on the other side of the fence. It is also small. Not the large, shaded, empty space she imagined from the satellite image.

She is close to giving up, but exits the lot, takes a left to the end of Lorong 18 and turns left twice again to return to 20. She drives up it slowly and turns into the first car park sign by Hotel 81. It is small and separated from Perfume Hotel by another fence. There are only three or four spaces. She manoeuvres out again, noticing another camera overlooking the lot and the entrance. Left again and she sees the entrance to the Perfume Rose Hotel parking space. It is the biggest hotel on the road and so should have a big car park, but her turns into the last two lots have revealed that the area between the two lorongs is a patchwork of fenced off yards, barely able to accommodate a couple of cars. Besides, it appears the Perfume Rose Hotel car park entrance is blocked by a no entry sign. It clearly has checks on who comes and goes. The upmarket end of Lorong 20 Geylang. This is not where the engineer's plastic packed body will be found.

She turns out onto Geylang Road again and drives home. It is time to take the dogs for a walk.

22. Crispy Fried Beef

It is Thursday night. They decide to go out because it's easier than staying in. He books an American-Chinese restaurant for 8 o'clock. The place does cocktails, they decide to meet in the restaurant bar at 7.30. She arrives by taxi a little early, and announces herself, their booking, and her intention to start with a drink while waiting for her company. She sits at a high table near the bar. There are mirrors on the walls and large vases with flower arrangements on tables spaced along the middle line of the oblong room, and on one side of the dining space there is an assortment of cakes, each kind under an enormous bell jar. The colours of the room are dark and the surfaces reflective. The place is almost empty and very cold. She orders a cocktail the clever name of which she instantly forgets. It contains longan and vodka and something purple and comes with a little gold leaf on top of a lot of crushed ice, served with a very thin black plastic straw. She sips her drink slowly through the straw. It has that longan taste that always reminds her of the smell of Chinese dry cleaners. She wonders if her brain is making an aromatic link or a cultural association.

She receives a message from him that he cannot find a cab and is walking and will be there in ten minutes. She plays with her phone for a while, avoiding the sense of being on her own and having nowhere to look. But the connection is bad, and she is getting tired of always staring at that screen. She realises that she likes sitting here on her own by the mirrors and sipping her cocktail through a very thin straw, so she puts the phone away and looks at her own reflection for a while. Her face and shoulders are looking thin, and she is satisfied. She watches the barman mixing drinks. He is wearing a white shirt and the sides of his head are shaved short while the longer hair on his head is in a little ponytail, mock-samurai-style. She notices the array of glasses hung above the bar. Hundreds of glasses, upside down, like a chandelier without lights. She looks at the two women sitting at a table in the restaurant. They are young and they are chatting, like good friends.

When he arrives, he is hot and there are beads of sweat on his forehead from walking through the heat outside. She has goosebumps on her arms from the cold inside, but the drink is making her feel it less. He orders a pisco sour but the waiter does not know what that is, and after going to ask at the bar brings back the cocktail menu. He chooses another drink with a witty name. It doesn't have gold leaf on the ice, but it also comes with a very thin black straw. He doesn't use it. She picks some of her gold leaf up with her straw and places it on her tongue and sticks it out at him. They smile at each other.

They move to a table by the window, taking what is left of their drinks with them, and have a look at the food menu. He asks for recommendations and the waiter lists far too many dishes, but they both pick out a favourite, orange crispy fried beef. There was a cheap noodle house near them in London many years ago which did takeaway boxes from the buffet. You paid at the till and got a foil box with a waxed paper lid. A sign by the till warned that you could only fill the box to the extent that the lid still fitted when you took it away. There was an all-you-can-eat buffet, but that cost more. They used to have a competition to see who could fit the most food in their box and still bend the foil edges around the lid. They weighed the boxes when they got home to find the winner. There was a technique to successfully packing the most fried rice, noodles, sweet and sour pork, beef in black bean sauce, cashew nut chicken and stir fry vegetables in the box and topping it up with spring rolls and hoisin duck pancakes and getting that lid on. A favourite dish to cram in with the others was sweet crispy fried beef.

They also order some duck and moo shu pancakes and chop suey and rice. When they finish their cocktails, they order two glasses of white wine; they have some sparkling water, too, as usual. The duck and the beef are very tasty, but the rest of the food is mediocre. There is too much fried food. They eat almost all of it anyway.

They don't seem to have much to say to each other over dinner.

They are both more tired that they think they should be at that hour. They decide to pay and go home. The bill comes with two fortune cookies. They haven't seen those in a while.

His fortune cookie says: 'Someone at this table has a secret you should know.' Her fortune cookie says, 'Forty-two.'

He smiles and says, 'The meaning of life.'

She smiles back at him and thinks about the body in the boot of her car.

The next morning she can't drive the dogs to their usual walking places, but takes them around the block. She cites a busy day as an excuse, will take them to the beach later, she murmurs as she kisses him goodbye, as if she needed to justify herself. She always leaves with the dogs as he gets ready for work, he's usually in the shower, or in front of the sink, shaving. She gets wet kisses or ones tinged with shaving foam. She likes these little banal rituals of married life. She always imagines, what if this is the last time I see him? and wants another kiss. It may be the last. Every morning she thinks, or at least half-thinks the same thing. He may die today, if I don't give him a goodbye kiss, another kiss, a last, third one, I will regret it forever. It is always his death she fears, never her own.

When she returns from the dog walk, she puts a pot of coffee on and prepares the dogs' breakfast. There is some cut up liver lung tripe mix in the fridge. She hopes to be able to get rid of the body in the boot of her car before lunch-time. After the dogs have finished and found their places of pre-noon repose (sofa, bed, dog bed, somewhere cool), she has a cup of coffee with soya milk. She opens up Google maps on the computer again and tries to find a very green space. There is an area between the Pierce reservoir and Upper Selatar reservoir that looks green and empty. It's part of the Central Catchment Nature Reserve. Sounds as organised as everything else in Singapore, but perhaps there is a corner of jungle where chaos reigns, where disintegration can find its own undisturbed place. There is a road, Old Upper Thompson Road, that loops into the forest and that on street view looks flanked by nothing but thick greenery for quite some distance. There also seems to be a hiking trail across the area, ending by the BKE. The Bukit Timah Expressway – she has to look it up, why is it not the BTE?

Looking, she comes across a news item: 'Decomposed body of a man found along BKE.' Why would you leave a body just off the highway? The body was discovered 'near a grass patch along BKE exit 10B towards Woodlands checkpoint.' Maybe he just died there? Some cans of beer were found next to the cadaver. The piece mentions 'a strong foul smell in the air,' and it makes her feel something, a feeling she cannot quite pin down. Inflections of nausea anxiety discomfort fear and a wish to flee. 'The body was highly decomposed, suggesting that the man had been dead for a few days.' So she has a few days, but she doesn't want to know how many. The body has only been in the car overnight, she doesn't even want to imagine it sitting in the heat for days. She wishes she had a wheelbarrow, so she could move the body deep into the forest. She cannot carry the engineer very far even though he isn't big. Drag him a little, perhaps, into some bushes. The hiking trail is out, then, it has to be accessible by car. Also, pedestrian traffic increases likelihood of early detection, she thinks. A place where cars drive but nobody walks is better. That's why that body was dumped by the BKE.

She wonders if dogs will eat human flesh. She has considered buying a meat grinder anyway, to make mince out of cheap cuts of meat for them. She has a quick look online. Somebody asks if a particular model will grind rabbit bones for the cat's dinner. Yes, it will grind rabbit and chicken bones. Human bones would take an industrial grinder. In Singapore in 1984 a man was allegedly killed and cooked into a curry by his wife and her brothers, 'with chilli and spices.' The human curry and rice were disposed of in bins around Singapore. She finds herself wondering why they threw away the curry. Why not serve it, eat it, like a South East Asian Sweeney Todd? Of course, nobody would question some left-over curry in a bin. Indeed, nobody ever did. The case only came to light through an informer. No murder weapon, body, or curry pot has ever been found. The whole thing may be fiction. How did they dismember him into pieces small enough for a curry? Apparently, a mutton seller was implicated. So, too many people were involved, somebody was bound to talk.

She will take the engineer to the woods alone, at night, and leave him somewhere he's unlikely to be found for a while. Drag him out of the boot along one of the quiet roads that bisect the planned pockets of wilderness in this city, where few venture out of their cars, afraid of mosquitos and snakes and worse. The last tiger was shot in Singapore in 1902, but wild pigs still roam both forests and roads of the northern parts of the island. Pigs eat everything. And wild dogs do, too. She will unroll him from his plastic packaging that is soiled with her sweat, and let nature do the cooking and the feasting.

She goes for a run. She can only ever run in the dark, early morning is dog time, going out later means hot sun already, she tried it only once. So the dogs are walked and fed around sunset, and then she runs. It took six months for her to even attempt running in the heat. She started as the first monsoon came in at the end of the year. A few degrees cooler, a little bit of wind. Nevertheless, she has to give in to the inevitable sweating, to accept that she becomes soaked and sticky. The hardest part is breathing. There is something about the humidity of the air, she thinks, that makes it harder to breathe, feels like the lungs are not getting enough oxygen even with deep breaths. Is it that the moisture actually displaces oxygen, or is it merely a sensation? Those born in Singapore, used to the constant heat, do they ever wish for fresh air? Cold, clear, crisp, mountain air.

The runs are slower, more torturous, than ever before. She had to start again with intervals of walking, slowly build up her running times, adding sprints. The fartlek makes it more varied, makes an inevitably dull activity a sport. The music helps, as does the backdrop of the central city lights as she runs along the river towards the bay. Makes it feel more significant, as if it had an important goal, heroic. Why? she wonders. Is it the association to countless film montages of the protagonist getting fit for the fight, Rocky-style, or are the montages themselves playing on a more deep rooted emotion? Music, rhythm, drums raising the spirits of troops and tribes, setting the shaman into his trance, making the jogger feel less suburban and more survivor. She returns drenched in sweat and does some bodyweight exercises and a few with dumbbells, push-ups, dips, squats, lunges, lifts for arms and shoulders.

He arrives home from work on his bike. She can hear him go around the house to put the bicycle out the back: at first the cleats on his shoes clomping on the drive, then the crunch of gravel as he wheels the bike through the pebbles covering the drains surrounding the patio. She unlocks the back door for him before he gets there, walks back into the kitchen, and resumes her exercises. Shoulder presses, lateral raises. Dumbbells up above her head, twelve times, out to the sides, twelve times. He comes in and stands by the kitchen island looking through the day's post as usual. She can see his straight, slender back, T-shirt sticking to his skin with sweat. His head is slightly bent at the neck, as he reads the papers in his hand, but his back remains straight as always. She thinks about swinging a dumbbell at his head. Would it be enough? The weights are not very heavy, and covered in rubber, but maybe it would knock him out? It would hurt his head, that is sure, and it makes her feel queasy to think about making him hurt.

'I'm going to have a shower,' he says.

'Ok,' she says.

23. The Chief

They go home for the first time fourteen months after they move. It's late September and the beginning of autumn in London, she can't wait to feel the freshness in the air, see the leaves changing colour, the golden light like a bittersweet syrup as the sun moves lower in the sky. She can't wait to wear proper clothes, jeans, jumpers, jackets, scarves, boots. Going for walks in the park (she will miss the dogs so much, but they have to be left behind for this short visit), then finding a cosy pub, outside chilly and inside warm just as it should be. They plan their two weeks carefully: a week of work in London for him, she visiting her parents for a few days, then a week off, seeing friends, pottering about town.

They arrive on the very early morning flight into grey skies over Heathrow. They have all the time in the world, so they take the tube into town, that interminable journey between rows and rows of brick terraces, in the bleak morning light. It feels like home. He has a room at the Savoy paid for by work, so they change at Piccadilly Circus and get off a stop later at Charing Cross. She notices the grime in the corners of the stairs and corridors of the underground, black soot and dirt accumulated over a century, the patina of all the life that has gone before. It feels comforting, like being part of something, a small cog in the huge machinery of this city stretching across time and space. They pull their suitcases along an empty early morning Strand. All shops and most cafes are still closed. In front of a pub someone is pouring water over the pavement. There is a faint smell of urine in the air. It's the morning after a Friday night. A homeless man sits in a doorway and screams something incomprehensible at them as they pass, and a light drizzle starts up. They laugh at the warm welcome London is extending, they have missed this. This feels real.

It is too early to check into their room, so they leave their cases at the hotel and wander up through Covent Garden as things start to open and the sun comes out. They have coffee and sweet buns, and reminisce. They walk all the way through Soho to Oxford Circus and back down to Leicester Square, popping into Hamley's, which they haven't visited in at least ten years. They feel like tourists in their own town and mess around with the toys and pick some presents out for the nieces they're going to see later.

After dropping their purchases back at the hotel, they catch the train from Charing Cross to their neighbourhood in South East London, going to the local Saturday food market a stone's throw from the old house. They meet some friends and chat to acquaintances they bump into by chance. She misses contact like this, chatting about nothing, noncommittally knowing you'll bump into each other again on the next dog walk or the one after that, and complaining about the weather. Familiar faces, familiar small talk. They have lunch from their favourite stall at the market, but it isn't quite as good as before, they've tweaked the recipe. She considers saying something but doesn't feel it's her place to do so anymore, she's not a regular customer, just a visitor passing through. In fourteen months' time the recipe will be different again.

Her mobile phone rings. Her mother. She is due to fly to Stockholm to see her parents in two days' time. She suddenly feels a little worried, but then thinks it's her mum wanting to make sure she buys something she believes she can only get from the UK, and therefore must remind her about now. But that is not it.

'Dad's in hospital. He had a pain in the rib, it got worse. So bad we called the ambulance. He screamed when I touched it. So he's in hospital,' her mother says.

'Ok, how is he now?' A stitch of worry, but she stays calm. She is good at staying calm under pressure.

'They did some x-rays; they found some changes.'

'So, what have they said?'

'They have found some changes, but he wants to go home. He's discharged himself, they have given him painkillers. He doesn't want to be in hospital when you come.'

'Is that a good idea? Where is he now?'

'I don't know, he's on his way home.'

'But he's ok, or what?'

'They found some changes. In his lungs.'

'I don't understand. What does that mean?'

Her mother's voice is different, she's rarely heard it this way. It's quiet but the intonation is like a scream.

'It's cancer. He's got cancer.'

'Is that what they said?'

'No, they're not saying.' But her mother knows, she's a senior medical doctor, semi-retired. She might be wrong, but she knows. 'Maybe it's COPD,' her mother adds, but she doesn't sound convinced. There and then they book a flight for the afternoon. It's still before midday, they have time to go to the hotel, pack a smaller bag, and head out to the airport again. This time they get the Heathrow Express. She spends the two weeks with her parents, he pops back to London for his working week but comes back again for the second seven days. Before that, on the Tuesday of the first week, when he is back in London and she is at her parents' house in Stockholm, her mother goes to work, one of the occasional days that she is called on to advise. Her mother still has access to the system, the repository of electronic patient journals.

She is home with her dad. Again, her mobile phone rings. Again, it's her mother. She's accessed her father's medical notes.

'Don't tell your dad,' her mother says.

It's not conclusive, of course, CT scans and biopsies are advised, but the 'changes' are described in his journal, in words that she doesn't quite understand but her mother does. There's not much chance of this being pulmonary disease. Signs of malignant neoplastic growth in lungs, masses commensurate with metastases in bone and liver, too.

'Don't tell your dad.'

But how can she not? She puts the phone down and thinks only for a minute. She can't sit here and make small talk over coffee knowing what she knows. Her dad is dying. And she is the one to break the news to him. That Tuesday afternoon she tells her father he has metastatic lung cancer.

She leaves Singapore so quickly, yet everything happens in slow-motion. Everyone is so understanding, so helpful, so enabling, it is as if the place and its people want to expel her, she thinks. Like a body getting rid of a foreign object, a splinter or piece of gravel. Irritating, encapsulated, ejected. The bursting of the boil. But the relief is all hers. The perfect excuse to escape, to cut short this sojourn in the heat, the ridiculously early morning dog walks, the overpriced and overpackaged supermarkets, the yoga and Pilates with all the other housewives, the lack of proper work, the goddam maids everywhere. Thank god. But why like this, god?

Of course she should go home and be with her father, no-one disputes that, they wonder why she has not already gone, why she takes the time she takes to sort things out. She cannot leave the dogs behind. It is expensive and complicated to ship two large dogs halfway across the world. What furniture should she take? The company couldn't be more understanding, of course his wife should move back, they arrange, they pay. The men that cocoon belongings turn up again. They pack up most things, except a few. He is staying back for a while to find a replacement, then joining her in London.

There is so much to sort out, but it is all sorted, and she is home before Christmas. It's as if she's never left, but everything is different. They do not pretend her father will have another Christmas.

She has never wished anyone dead as much as she wishes her father dead those months. For the gestation period of a human being, nine months, she watches him pass away. He says he is not afraid of dying, but she does not believe him. He tries chemo for a few months, and radiotherapy too when the cancer spreads to his brain. There's some success as far as one can speak of success when inevitable death is held at bay for who knows how long, possibly a month or two, maybe only a couple of weeks. He seems relieved when she finally tells him she's not sure he should continue with the treatment. That she's spoken to mum and she doesn't want it either. Her mother had not said, because how do you tell someone you have loved for five decades that you'd rather they died. He did not want to hurt her, because how do you tell your wife of fifty years you just want it to end.

She asks if he wants to go to Switzerland. A mountain holiday? It can be arranged. Too clinical, he says, and the Swiss, he's not sure he can stand the Swiss. He is still laughing about it, it's early, he still manages to walk his dog up and down the path outside the house almost every day. Later he tells her he wishes that someone could just take the decision out of his hands, like the Chief. You know? he says. She's not sure she knows, but she nods. Native American senicide? A sacred place, the elder chieftain asks to be left to die. No, her father is asking not to decide. Ubasute, carry your mother up the mountain. Ättestupa, push daddy off a cliff. It is weeks before she realises which Chief he is talking about. Chief Broom. When the fog finally lifts, he puts a pillow to McMurphy's lobotomised head, rips the symbol of control out of the bathroom floor and smashes his way to freedom, following the geese. One flew east, one flew west, one flew over the cuckoo's nest.

He has two weeks left to live, but she doesn't know it yet. He is still at home, receiving hospital care. Nurses and doctors come and go. He is so weak, it is close to the end, but he asks how long, and she cannot answer. They ask the doctors, and they cannot answer. Weeks, not months, they say. She trawls the internet for last days of life, signs that death is near. She wants to know, she wants a number, days, hours, she can't stand watching anymore. He sees things that are not there, a common experience at the very end of life. People see dead relatives if they believe. He doesn't, but he asks if she can see the 'them' in the room too. Sometimes he sees a single figure, sometimes multitudes, he says that some he knows, some he doesn't. Once he beckons as if to a dog.

Her mother says he's asked once, for pills, to die. But her mother had answered there were none. She researches what drugs it takes to kill a man. Finds suicide sites, overdose information, but no answers. The ranges, from poisoning to overdose to fatal quantity, are massive. To be sure you need a very large dose of something. There are plenty of pills in the house, opiates, benzos. If she ground them all up and made him swallow, would he die? Would the death be better or worse than the one he is about to experience?

Almost all the information she finds describes a patient that drifts in and out of consciousness, sleeping more and more, until, finally, they do not wake. The doctor says, its usually undramatic, death. You simply fall asleep. He's been told that before, at the beginning when he was diagnosed, and he wanted to know. That's what they said. You go to sleep. He starts sleeping less. He doesn't want to go to sleep. She finds one article that mentions the other path to death, the hard one. Less common, but not unusual when brain tumours are present. The one nobody speaks about.

He doesn't drift to sleep at home. He tries to run away from death. He is so thin, so wasted, she is surprised at the force she needs to use to hold him down in bed, to stop him standing up and falling over. He doesn't know where he wants to go. To follow the geese? When the nurse has to come every two hours, with the biggest syringe she's seen, emptying it into the catheter in his arm to give him a couple of hours of peace, she persuades her mother that they cannot keep him at home anymore. When he next wakes, tries to take his clothes off, tries to flee, her mother sits next to him on the bed. She holds his hand, calls his name. He looks blankly at her. Her mother is satisfied, this is what she's waited for, he no longer knows.

He is given propofol in hospital. Sometimes, they say, not even tranquilizers work, anaesthesia is the only thing left. She sits next to his hospital bed counting his breaths, taking time. How many per minute? She reads the internet pages on the last moments of life again and again. How long? The doctor has said he could die at any moment. He doesn't die for days. They ask the nurse. How long? How long have you seen? Two weeks. She is filled with horror. For him, for her mother, for herself. She can't take much more of this, neither can her mum. After weeks of not sleeping, they are relieved that they can go home, sleep, eat. She feels guilty, they leave him there, but they must live. He is dying so slowly.

He looks a little worried one morning, they tell her they lowered the propofol because his breathing slowed. He got a bit agitated. They raised the dose somewhat again, but not too much.

'We don't want to give him so much he stops breathing, do we?' the doctor, a hard middle-aged woman, says, with a smile.

She is stunned, stares. She wants to say, 'surely that is exactly what we want!' She says nothing. But the next day she breaks down in tears before another doctor, a younger, softer woman. It's the doctor's turn to stare. She tries to explain to the doctor, but she is not sure she is succeeding. The doctor seems scared she is complaining about his care. No, no its excellent, but... again, she doesn't say, it's too much, stop it please, please, just let him go. Help him, help us. She can't ask, she knows the doctors can't say, can't do. It's a crime, they have careers.

When the doctor is gone, she sits down next to him again, counts breaths. Looks at his fingernails, feels his hands and forehead. Is he turning a bit pale? His face is so drawn, his features sharp. Head tilted back and mouth open, and he keeps drawing breaths, rarely but regularly. She listens for the rattle. Could she put a pillow over his face?

She looks at the drip into his arm, follows the slender tube with its milky white fluid with her gaze to the bag suspended above the bed. In between there's a machine, blinking lights, a number. Regulating the flow, buttons: + and -. What if she pressed the plus? Just a little, or a lot. It would be so easy. Surely, he would simply fall into a deeper sleep. Like the dog, isn't an overdose of anaesthetic what they gave the dog? Would anyone notice? Then she imagines him going into fits, personnel rushing in, pointing accusingly at her.

He said, he wished the Chief would. A pillow. But she can't.

Epilogue

The time of golden light, the mildness of air, and the sweet sadness of late summer is over. Now the grey clouds are moving in, mornings stay strangely dark even when the sun has risen, shaded by layer and layer of vapour in the atmosphere. The air feels damp, and the cold creeps closer to the skin. It's almost time for hats and gloves, but not quite. She is sure she leaves it later, lower temperature wise, in autumn before protecting the extremities, than when they are bared again in the spring. Not wanting to accept the fact of winter, slow to believe the truth of summer.

They are walking in the park: the skyline of the Isle of Dogs across the river, the dome to the right, and on the left and further away, the old and new peaks of the city. They wander among the trees, brown now. There has been a chestnut plague, so many leaves never had their celebration of the approaching end, just withered in the late summer and now they droop, still attached, dry or damp with rain, eventually they'll fall and cover the earth. Mulch doesn't care what colour you were in life. What you did or thought. They walk down the gulley by the old oak stump, and she stops a while to let the old hound rest, to let the young one hunt, to say hello to the little dead one whose ashes she spread there.

Some weeks after they had decided to move to Singapore, she had realised she had to take a decision about the ashes. Her immediate instinct was that she must take them. She couldn't just throw the little one away before leaving! About a week later, she understood that the time to scatter the ashes was now, a few months before moving, doing it for its own sake. The place was given, Greenwich Park – the home of the best squirrel chasing in South East London. She even knew the place, the dip they called Squirrel Valley, that is where the little one belonged. She cried when she spread the ashes, and part of her wanted to scream No! Come back! and gather the ashes from the wet grass, scraping them up with her cold fingers, stuffing them back into the cardboard tube, taking them back to the vets, picking up the little one alive two weeks later, when the arrow of time was reversed by the power of grief alone.

Now they are back together, back where they belong. The ashes of our dead is what connects us to the earth of our home. She thinks of her father's ashes, spread on a wooded hilltop, far away, yet so much closer than she has been for the past couple of years. Nothing keeps us in place like death, while life is movement and change. To move away is to stay alive. To return, to settle, is to accept death. She wants nothing more than to stop running.

Since they have been back the girl has learned to stalk. She never did before, has she finally figured it out, or is it age, slowing her down and forcing her to be wiser, more cunning? She stands, proud, ears alert, sniffing the air, then suddenly her head drops to form a line with her spine, so still. She moves her paws, one at a time, underneath her body, taut. Eyes fastened on her quarry, the closer she gets the slower she goes. She seems to be calculating the distance between the squirrel and the trees, waiting until the creature makes a move, exposing itself in the void. She is only metres away, stopped now. Then the decision, to go, to pounce, to kill. She leaps forward, only a few bounds to the prey. Usually squirrels scamper, their little bodies turn so much faster than the dog's, and they disappear up trees. But this time the girl gets lucky.

She'd rather not have to dispatch a squirrel today, she really doesn't want to, she's not wearing any gloves. But she needn't worry. The animal hangs limply in the hound's mouth. One shake of the body anchored in her maw on four canines, an instinctive jerk of the head, a skill she was born with, and the squirrel is dead.

ACKNOWLEDGEMENTS

First of all, thank you Clara Chow, without whose insistence that I write 500 words a day this book would never have come into being, and for, together with Christine Lee and Yen Yen Wu, being my small tribe of likeminded people in Singapore.

A massive thank you to my early readers, of parts and whole, for your feedback and support: Hannah Nicholls, Danielle Sands, Anna Synenko, Katie Willis, Kate Armstrong, Duncan White and especially Oliver Belas for his on-the-money suggestions. Thank you Robert Eaglestone for always having my back even when you hadn't read a word of this novel.

Thank you to Robert Peett for understanding what I was trying to do with this book, and believing in it enough to publish it, and to my agent Philippa Sitters for being the best cheerleader.

Special thanks to Hannah again, and Thom Webb, for being there last thing when we left and first thing when we came back.

And thank you Marcus Cheadle for believing in me more than I believed in myself.

London, July 2022

An Island
Karen Jennings
LONGLISTED FOR THE 2021 BOOKER PRIZE

'...a moving, transfixing novel ... rendered in majestic and extraordinary prose.' Booker Prize Judges panel.

'This is a book that gives us faith that the Booker prize judges are doing their job...' John Self, The Times.

'An Island is a small but powerful book, with the reach of a more capacious work, compounding merciless political critique and allegory rendered in tender prose.' Catherine Taylor, The Guardian

'A gripping, terrifying and unforgettable story.' Elleke Boehmer

Samuel has lived alone for a long time; one morning he finds the sea has brought someone to offer companionship and to threaten his solitude...

A young refugee washes up unconscious on the beach of a small island inhabited by no one but Samuel, an old lighthouse keeper. Unsettled, Samuel is soon swept up in memories of his former life on the mainland: a life that saw his country suffer under colonisers, then fight for independence, only to fall under the rule of a cruel dictator; and he recalls his own part in its history. In this new man's presence he begins to consider, as he did in his youth, what is meant by land and to whom it should belong. To what lengths will a person go in order to ensure that what is theirs will not be taken from them?

A novel about guilt and fear, friendship and rejection; about the meaning of home.

Karen is a South African author. Her debut novel, Finding Soutbek, was shortlisted for the inaugural Etisalat Prize for African Fiction. Her memoir, Travels with my Father, was published in 2016. She was winner of the K. Sello Duiker Memortial Literary Award 2021 by the SA Literary Awards in 2021.

Her next novel, Crooked Seeds, will be published jointly by Holland House Books in the UK and Hogarth Press in the USA in 2024.

The Feeling House
Saleh Addonia

"a vital project illuminating the realities of human beings on the move across this restless planet,"*Ian McMillan, Poet & Presenter of BBC Radio 3's 'The Verb'*

A young girl awakes alone next to a burning truck and befriends a nearby cloud; an Eritrean refugee studies interior design as he attempts to build his new home; a group of illegal immigrants embark on an arduous journey in the city as they desperately seek: Her. Darting from the dark underbelly of London to the sexually impenetrable home, Saleh Addonia writes stories of displacement and frustration. Tinged with isolation and alienation, each tale strikes the imagination as Addonia weaves the surreal into devastatingly human stories.

Saleh Addonia was born in Eritrea from an Eritrean mother and an Ethiopian Father. As a child, he survived the Om Hajar massacre and migrated to Sudan. He grew up in refugee camps where he lost his hearing at the age of 12. Addonia spent his early teens in Saudi Arabia and arrived in London as an 18 year old refugee.

Three Days By The Sea
Helen E. Mundler

No-one talks about Susie but no-one can forget her – until Gina and Robert receive invitations to a family reunion by the sea in Cornwall. As the three days unfold, the stories and secrets of each character are mapped against England's changing society through the history of the family. Gradually, the truth of Susie's disappearance over twenty years ago is revealed as the secrets, griefs, and eccentricities of one family are exposed to the Cornish light.

Three Days by the Sea is a subtle, funny and moving story of hope and renewal. With dry, sharp humour and warmth, Helen Mundler unpicks the trials and tensions of family life.

Helen E. Mundler has published two other novels, *Homesickness* (Dewi Lewis, 2003) and *L'Anglaise* (Holland House, 2018), as well as three critical works, *Intertextualité dans l'oeuvre* d'A.S.Byatt (Paris, Harmattan, 2003), *The Otherworlds of Liz Jensen: a Critical Reading* (Boydell and Brewer, Rochester, USA, 2016), and *The Noah Myth in Twenty-First-Century Novels: Rewritings from a Drowning World* (Boydell and Brewer, Rochester, USA, 2022).

Rescuing Barbara
by Cass McMain

Ignoring her mother may have been a mistake.

During a bout of sobriety, Barbara implored her young daughter to turn her back on her if she began drinking again. Exhausted by her mother's alcoholism, Cass McMain finally took this advice and ignored everything the woman said or did for many years. She did not return calls, she did not visit, she did not react, send letters, or cajole. She simply turned away and waited for her mother to hit bottom or die trying. But as she discovered, bottom may be much farther down than one expects. Eventually, she is forced to wade in and untangle the mess her mother has created.

A gripping series of moments – painful, loving, desperate –*Rescuing Barbara*is a bitterly funny, and even lyrical true story about the inherent dangers of detachment ... and a reminder that predators are everywhere, waiting to fill in the gaps.

Cass McMainwas born in Albuquerque and raised in the far North Valley, among the cottonwoods.

The Bellboy
Anees Salim

Latif's life changes when he is appointed bellboy at the Paradise Lodge – a hotel where people come to die. After his father's death, drowned in the waters surrounding their small Island, it is 17 year-old Latif's turn to become the man of the house and provide for his ailing mother and sisters. Despite discovering a dead body on his first day of duty, Latif finds entertainment spying on guests and regaling the hotel's janitor, Stella, with made-up stories. However, when Latif finds the corpse of a small-time actor in Room 555 and becomes a mute-witness to a crime that happens there, the course of Latif's life is irretrievably altered.

At the age of sixteen, Anees Salim dropped out of school and left home to become a writer. He travelled across India and worked as a bellboy, waiter, shop assistant and ghost writer before joining advertising. He currently works as a Creative Director with FCB India. His published works include *Vanity Bagh*(winner of The Hindu Literary Prize for Best Fiction 2013), *The Blind Lady's Descendants*(winner of the Raymond Crossword Book Award for Best Fiction 2014 and the Kendra Sahitya Akademi Award 2018),*The Small-town Sea*(winner of the Atta Galatta-Banaglore Literature Festival Book Prize for Best Fiction 2017), and *The Odd Book of Baby Names*. His works have been translated into French, German, and several Indian languages.

The Death Script
Ashutosh Bhardwaj

A haunting ode to those who paid the ultimate price—through the prism of the Maoist insurgency, Ashutosh Bhardwaj meditates on larger questions of violence and betrayal, love and obsession, and what it means to live with and write about death.

From 2011 to 2015, Ashutosh lived in the Red Corridor in India wherein the Ultra-Left Naxalites, taking inspiration from the Russian revolution and Mao's tactics, work to overthrow the Indian government by the barrel of the gun. He made several trips thereafter reporting on the insurgents, on police and governmental atrocities, and on the lives caught in the crossfire. The Death Script chronicles his experiences and bears witness to the lives and deaths of the unforgettable men and women he meets from both sides of the struggle, bringing home the human cost of conflict with astonishing power. Narrated in multiple voices, the book is a creative biography of the region, Dandakaranya, that combines the rigour of journalism, the intimacy of a diary, the musings of a travelogue, and the craft of a novel.

The Death Script is one of the most significant works of non-fiction to be published in India in recent times, bringing often overlooked perspectives and events to light with empathy and searing clarity. Praised by scholars and critics, the book has won many awards.

Ashutosh Bhardwaj is a bilingual journalist, fiction writer and literary critic. He experiments with prose in various forms and genres.As a journalist, he has traveled across Central India and documented the conditions of tribes caught in the conflict between the Maoist insurgents and the police, and investigating encounter killings political corruption, and electoral malpractice. He is the only journalist in India to have won the prestigious Ramnath Goenka Award for Excellence in Journalism for four consecutive years. In 2015, he was shortlisted for the Reuters' Kurt Schork Awards in International Journalism.